TENNESSEE MOONLIGHT

by

Violet L. Ryan

WHISKEY CREEK PRESS
www.whiskeycreekpress.com

Published by
WHISKEY CREEK PRESS

Whiskey Creek Press
PO Box 51052
Casper, WY 82605-1052
www.whiskeycreekpress.com

ISBN 978-1-60313-213-8

Credits
Cover Artist: Jinger Heaston
Editor: Melanie Billings

Printed in the United States of America

Dedication

~~To family and friends who read my work and offered encouragement.~~

Prologue

When moonlight bathes the Tennessee night with its luminous rays, the glow is like a soft morning sun peeking from behind the mountains. On a night like that, Ann Mason slipped out the back door of her little mountain cabin, leaving a drunken husband looking for his favorite punching bag. She had managed to avoid Red's fists for the last hour, and she knew he stood on the verge of passing out. That was always the most dangerous time, the time when he usually did the most damage, the time when she tried to make herself scarce.

She didn't always succeed. Many times she spent several days with a face that looked like hamburger, not to mention all the bruises hidden beneath her clothing. Once, she ended up in the doctor's office so he could set a broken arm. She had a lot of scars. Most of them were on the inside, and they were deeper and uglier than the ones on the outside.

She'd sweet-talked Red's dog into the house and gave the ferocious mutt her own meager supper, which she'd saved for just that purpose. She escaped into the night before he finished wolfing down his rare treat. That's how she managed to sneak out. That dog had given her away more times than she could count. Brutus hated her almost as much as Red did, except when he wanted something to eat. Like master, like dog.

She had her dog with her now. She'd raised Peanut, the only thing in the world that loved her, from a pup. The night she found him, she'd ventured out for a moonlit walk. Along the road, she heard a car and ducked out of sight because she didn't want anyone seeing her new bruises. She caught a glimpse of something flying out the door of a moving vehicle. After the automobile passed, she heard pitiful puppy cries and moved to investigate. He seemed so little when she first saw him, ergo the name, but he grew into a big strong dog that even Brutus gave way to.

He was almost six months older than Red's dog; otherwise, he probably wouldn't have survived puppyhood. Red taught Brutus viciousness from the day he brought him home, whereas she raised Peanut to love and protect. Of course, she encouraged those traits without Red's awareness. He would never have allowed her to succeed if he'd known. Peanut stood up to Brutus and showed him he would fight if necessary, and win, so Brutus respected him.

Now they were moving quickly and quietly through territory Ann had known since childhood. She'd lived there all her life, first with her father, Jessie Randall, who'd also been an abuser, then with her husband, Red, the man her father gave her to. Her mother died when she was very young. Ann strongly suspected Jessie beat her to death, but as far as she knew, he'd never been accused of the crime.

They were near the old lake road when Peanut stopped and stood dead still. She followed suit, completely trusting her dog's instincts and hearing, knowing they were much keener than hers. As they silently listened, Ann heard the faint, but unmistakable sounds of scuffling, then fists hitting flesh and groans of pain.

As her ears tuned in to the night sounds, she could hear heavy breathing, a sound she often heard from Red as he exerted himself to beat the crap out of her. Then she heard mocking laughter, the same kind that came from Red when he finished pounding on her and she was only semi-conscious. Someone was getting a beating!

Her eyes were adjusting just as her ears were. Through brush and weeds as tall as her head, she made out a group of men moving, arms and fists raised and lowered with speed as feet kicked viciously. She felt sick. Peanut recognized the sounds as well and emitted a low growl. Ann put her hand on him and shushed him almost silently, afraid she might be heard. She didn't want the wrath of these vile brutes falling on her head.

A sound split the night. It might have been a branch falling from a tree, it could have been an animal crashing through the undergrowth, but whatever it was brought an abrupt halt to the violence Ann grudgingly witnessed. With unthinking mob mentality, the men ran for an unseen vehicle, revved the engine, and sped away into the night like the cowards they truly were.

Ann listened in the sudden silence. Dare she move? She waited another minute but heard nothing. Almost too afraid to budge, she parted the weeds and slowly crept forward. Less than twenty feet from where she'd stood listening, she spied a lump on the ground. The bright Tennessee moonlight allowed her to identify the shape as a human being, but that was about all. She sat well out of reach, uncertain if approaching would be safe, and watched to see if the lump would move. She stayed alert to the surrounding area in case this person's "friends" returned.

One minute passed, then two. Feeling antsy, she moved a little closer. Nothing happened. Ann shifted even closer, but the lump didn't move, and she couldn't hear it breathing. She leaned in and hesitantly put forth a hand to touch what appeared to be a shoulder. No reaction.

She noted the size and decided the form looked too big for a woman—must be a man. She'd had only bad experiences with men. Ann didn't want him waking up and deciding he would take his frustrations out on her. She already had enough of that.

After an interminable amount of time passed, Ann worked up the courage to try taking his pulse. Nerves jumped as she reached out a finger, but he didn't move or make a sound when she touched his neck. She felt the slight throbbing of his heartbeat, which seemed so weak even she recognized the danger of his situation.

He needed help, but no one lived nearby. Ann didn't have a phone, she couldn't drive, and with any luck at all Red would have passed out cold by now, which would be a good thing. If he were still awake, he'd probably finish off the poor old lump. That left Ann. Assessment of his injuries proved impossible even in the bright moonlight. She must move him somewhere that had electricity available, but where? And how?

Ann possessed a good brain, and from lack of options, she had always worked out her own problems. Instantly, she thought of the hen house. One spring she ran an extension cord out to the rickety building to keep her baby chicks from freezing during an early cold snap. Red never went there because the chickens were her job. That's where she would put the injured stranger.

Now, how? She remembered the old tarpaulin covering the tractor. If she could roll him onto the tarp, maybe she could drag him to the hen house. She ran home, slowing as she neared the cabin and peeking in a window. Yeah, Red had passed out with all the lights on. He'd blame her when he woke up, saying she wasted electricity and cost him money. As if he earned any, anyway. She sold the eggs after she cared for the chickens all year. She also took the vegetables to market after she planted, weeded, harvested, and cleaned them. The only work Red did consisted of climbing on the tractor in the spring, when the engine would start, and plowing the ground. Oh, and he eagerly spent her money on moonshine.

With Brutus still locked in the house, it seemed safe to collect the tarp and hurry back to the lump. Her instincts told her the man would die without help, and she didn't think he would last very long.

He remained positioned exactly the way she'd left him. Ann spread the tarp beside him and rolled the man onto the heavy canvas. Though she still felt afraid, compassion overcame fear. She identified strongly with this unfortunate soul. She had to help him.

Pulling the battered man back to the hen house proved a difficult job for a small female like Ann, but she was strong from the hard work she'd always done, so she managed it an inch at a time. After she dragged him inside, she rolled him onto an old blanket, an extra one she kept in the shack for the times she spent the night out there avoiding Red's fists. When she finished, she quickly replaced the tarp.

Ann returned, flicked on the light, and took her first good look at her charge. He was a black man, maybe sixty give or take a few years, but he looked older. His crinkly black hair and beard were peppered with white. He obviously hadn't been eating regularly. Even though he was a large man, he appeared to be nothing but skin and bones, which explained why she'd been able to drag him back home. He looked a bloody mess. The gory sight didn't alarm Ann too much. Her own face sometimes looked like that. She would know more when she cleaned the blood off.

She tiptoed into the barn for liniment and alcohol, also collecting soap and the clean rags she'd put out there just yesterday. Water from the pump would have to do. It would be cold, but clean. Praise God! He always provided.

Ann spent the next few hours removing filthy, bloody clothes, washing wounds, applying alcohol and liniment, binding his chest, and redressing him in his own dirty rags so he wouldn't know she'd seen his scrawny naked body.

But she had seen it, and the damage proved extensive. His skin was light enough that Ann could see rapidly developing bruises covered most of his body. There were too many scrapes and cuts to count. His attackers had broken his nose, and in her opinion, some of his ribs were cracked, at the very least. She hoped it was trauma and shock that kept him unconscious, not the head wound. Ann wouldn't let herself think about what she would do if he died.

She fixed him up the best she could, and sat back to wait and see if he would awake. It didn't take long. A few minutes after she finished, he moaned and began to shake. She piled straw, dry cleaning rags, and her old jacket on top of him and sat helplessly by when that didn't look as if it would be enough to warm him. An eternity slipped away before the shaking stopped, and he started to perspire. She bathed his face and arms with cold water until he quieted and fell into a restful sleep just before sun-up. Finally, Ann slept, too.

Chapter 1

Five years later...

Jackson Barrister flew down the highway as fast as the Tennessee hills would allow. He was mad. He was fuming! The argument with his dad kept replaying over and over in his mind.

"Jack, it's gotta stop! It's gotta stop right now! What's wrong with you, Son? Why can't you find a decent woman and settle down? God knows you're old enough. Your brother's two years your junior, and he has three kids." Mike Barrister paced from one side of his huge office to the other. Mike did his thinking that way. And right then, he thought he would enjoy throttling his eldest son.

"You've forgotten what it's like to be young," Jack felt motivated to say. "You sowed your share of wild oats, or so I've been told." That elicited an unwanted reaction from the older man.

"Don't ever compare my youthful shenanigans with the things you're doin'," Mike yelled. When he became really stirred up, he tended to drop his fifty dollar college words and revert to his dad's earthier language. "I had respect for the fairer sex. You just mow 'um down. Not only do you not respect 'um, you don't even like 'um. But this latest affair is the last straw. I told you to stay away from that girl, but would you listen? No. She's only eighteen and the daughter of a good client. Used to be, anyway."

"Now, wait a minute. Don't go painting that little number innocent. She knew exactly what she wanted," Jack defended himself. "And I didn't take a thing she wasn't dying to give." Jack grew almost as angry as his father. That little baggage had chased him all over town until he gave in just to get rid of her. Afterward, Gina Lambert ran to Mama and cried big crocodile tears, hoping to trap him into marriage. No way. But what chance did he have of convincing the rest of the world the girl's bad morals weren't his fault if his own father didn't believe him? The look on Dad's face said he didn't.

"Yes, I suppose that's the real problem," Mike murmured thoughtfully. "You've always had everything handed to you without ever having to put forth any effort. Even the money you lavish on your 'entertainment' is paid into your account whether you do a lick of work or not." Mike trained his dark brown eyes on his eldest until Jack started to feel woolly worms dancing in his belly. Mike didn't wait a minute longer before he leaned forward and delivered a dreadful verdict.

"Boy, you're breaking Mama's heart, and I tell you, it's gotta stop. And I'm the one who's gonna stop it."

At that instant, Jack feared Dad's declaration didn't bode well for him. "Take it easy, Dad." Belatedly, Jack thought to use a little of his famous charm. "I understand how you feel." That assertion brought another unwelcome response.

"Do you?" Mike narrowed his eyes. "I'm not sure you do, but I am sure you're about to find out." He stopped pacing and returned to his desk, seating his long, slightly rotund body in his overstuffed office chair. He leaned back in his master-of-all-I-survey position and stared at Jack intently, taking stock of the handsome young man.

Mike felt proud of his son, and with good reason. Jack, still in his prime at twenty nine, stood a quarter inch short of six feet. Superbly built with wide shoulders, narrow hips, and long legs—Jack was all lean, hard muscle. He had a narrow face, a straight nose, and a wide mouth with full lips. His hair was dark sable brown, and his eyes were the color of rich, hot chocolate. Women found him irresistible. Usually his father did, too, but not that day. Mike had gazed at Jack until he felt uneasy, then Dad shook his head, sighed, and informed the younger man of his shocking decree.

"I've been remiss with you, Son, and it's high time I corrected my mistake." Mike shuffled a few papers until he found the one he wanted and handed the memo to Jack. "That nice automatic payment that goes into your bank account every month is terminated as of today." He continued talking right over the gasp that erupted from Jack's wide open mouth. "From now on you'll be punching a time clock just like the rest of my employees. You'll be paid according to the job you're actually doing."

Jack tried to object, but he barely sputtered before Mike continued.

"You'll be starting under old Dan Weaver. He's putting together a project I've been planning for five years. The change in status will transfer you out of town for a while and away from this latest mess you've created. Maybe, just maybe, it'll remind you of the values you seem to have lost over the years." Mike looked at his oldest son with a suspicious sheen in his eyes, but his firm voice told Jack there might be tenderness in his sire, but no softness.

That had been two months ago. Okay, maybe he deserved punishment. His lifestyle definitely leaned a little toward the wild side. Somewhere along the road, Jack joined up with a group of rich kids who had a taste for decadence. He couldn't say now why he started hanging out with them. Their actions weren't his style, at least not in the beginning. He couldn't remember exactly when he started treating women like toys instead of people, sex objects to be used and thrown away. He hadn't been aware of the change in himself until that confrontation with Mike. He still had trouble believing he'd behaved as badly as his dad thought.

He hadn't been using drugs, but he did drink way too much. And he'd been gambling. That one he couldn't deny.

He couldn't deny the womanizing either. Still, he didn't feel his way of life warranted being exiled to the backwoods of...where was he? Tennessee. That sounded right.

Okay, he did deserve banishment, but he didn't have to like it. He'd done his best to talk Dad out of his decision, and Jack's best had always been pretty good, but Mike wouldn't budge an inch. Jack didn't want to give up his position with the family company. He liked the perks a boss's son often enjoyed. If he couldn't convince his dad to back down and reinstate him, he might be forced to look for another playground. Maybe a few words from the fathers of his friends would influence Mike's decision. After Dad cooled off, he'd try reasoning with him. If that didn't work, he'd call in some favors.

So there he sat, behind the wheel of his hunter green Jaguar, racing up and down the winding roads of rural Tennessee toward a hick town called Andersonville. He hurtled toward an unknown fate inflicted on him for the purpose of shaping his character and straightening him out.

Jack had to admit the surroundings were beautiful. Spring had sprung. Wild flowers covered the fields all around him. Trees sprouted tender new leaves so pure a shade of green it would inspire poetry, if you were able to rhyme two words, which he couldn't. Though he recognized the loveliness of northeastern Tennessee, Jack found enjoyment of the scenery difficult when he faced months of imprisonment there in the hills.

Development of a piece of land along the shores of Norris

Lake had become his new on-the-job training. He considered the area charming and busy, even at that time of year. Fishing there purported to be first-class. He'd also been told the water sports were a top draw in summer months. He didn't plan on staying around long enough to check it out, but he decided knowing a smidgen about the area before he faced old Dan would be a good idea. With that in mind, he drove on past Norris, toward the town located closest to the site where Barrister's planned on building their resort.

He rounded yet another curve, and there before him stood Andersonville. The tiny borough consisted of a few houses, a church, a cemetery, and a trading post/variety store. Jack groaned. What on earth would he do for entertainment there at the end of nowhere? He had his work cut out for him if he intended being home before summer.

Jack turned around and headed for the Super 8 Motel in Norris where Dan Weaver had arranged a meeting between them. On the drive back, he considered his situation. After serving as his own boss all those years, Jack found the prospect of reporting to another person mortifying. But he supposed if he must answer to someone, Dan would be the best one.

He checked in and picked up a message from the older man to meet him on site. Dan had given explicit directions, and Jack discovered he needed them. In spite of good instructions, he managed to lose his way twice.

On one of those occasions, he spotted a small house with

several outbuildings and a person working some ground he assumed would be a garden. The individual looked like a plain woman dressed in baggy overalls and a long sleeved work shirt. She'd stuffed an old brown hat on her head and wore gumboots on her feet. She could've been a man, but two things suggested differently. She looked very small, and the breeze blowing against her chest gave a hint of curves. Definitely female, but definitely not his type! Jack tried to envision any one of the women he dated dressed that way. Not in their lifetime. They'd all slit their wrists before they'd let anyone see them like that.

After a couple of false tries, he found the lakeside site where Dad expected him to spend the next few months "becoming a man," unless he could convince Mike he'd matured enough to return to the city. The property proved very appealing. He'd seen the preliminary plans, and now he visualized how beautiful the resort would look when they completed the complex.

He swerved into the narrow gravel path that served as a drive, killed the engine, and hopped out. There, parked in an undersized clearing surrounded by forest, sat a small trailer with his family's company logo printed on the side. A Chevy truck sat beside it. That probably meant Dan had already arrived. Jack knocked on the door and entered without waiting for a response.

Dan was fifty-one years old, but he looked seventy, which might be the reason everyone called him "old" Dan

Weaver. He was heavily built, not fat, but broad, muscled, and fairly tall, very stout. He had hair white as sugar and combed straight back from his forehead. His face was leathery-looking and as lined as a road map. His brandy-colored eyes were sharp and clear, and when you looked deep into them, you'd swear he was no more than thirty.

"Morning, Jackson," Dan greeted his new problem.

Dan's casual address irritated the younger man, making him feel as if he were an underling instead of the son and heir. "Dan," he acknowledged, trying and failing to put the older man in his place.

Dan looked him over, noting his belligerent stance and defensive attitude. He'd been warned by Daddy. The boy wasn't happy about being there. Somehow, teaching the kid a lesson had become his job. Taking care of their own mistakes should be a vocation reserved for the parents. Dan wasn't any happier about this situation than Jackie-boy.

"Your father tells me you're interested in learning how to put a project together from the bottom up." Dan kept such a straight face that he fooled Jack into believing Mike hadn't related the real reason he sent his son to Tennessee.

"Yes," Jack replied, and as an afterthought he added, "Dad says you're the best person for that." Jack felt certain the old man would eat up a compliment coming from the boss's son. He'd been hanging out with people who would fall for exactly that type of thing, but the leathered old man just stared at him with resignation.

"I've set up this trailer for your living quarters," Dan began, putting into motion the first stage of a plan for Jackson Barrister's reformation.

"I've already checked into the motel in town." Jack's reply, and the grimace on his face, underlined his distaste for the aluminum box.

"I need you out here," old Dan said, sober-faced as a judge. "We've had an incident or two, and I've decided someone on site twenty-four hours every day might be a deterrent."

Jack immediately bristled.

"Why me?" he practically shouted. "You're the expert!" He spat the word out, making the praise an insult when it should have been a tribute. "You staying out here would make a lot more sense. You can handle problems a novice like me couldn't possibly understand." Jack puffed up with pride. He widened his stance, straightened his back, and looked down his superior nose at Dan, certain the old man wouldn't recognize sarcasm when he heard it. Jack was wrong, but Dan proved way too clever to let the young pup see into his mind, so he played along.

"No, you're the best person for the job. You're an owner and a family member, so you have authority that I don't. Besides, a warm body is all we really need." Dan applied a little sarcasm of his own. "You can handle that, can't you?"

Jack sputtered a bit more, but he soon recognized Dan's determination. He dropped back into his Jaguar and headed for the motel without paying attention to the instructions the site supervisor tried to pass on. He would've done well if he'd stayed and listened, but he became stupid with arrogance and way too full of himself for any common sense. As a result, he drove away without knowing what kind of attacks Dan Weaver would've described.

Jack arrived back at his room and immediately called his parent's home. When he asked to speak with his father, the housekeeper told him Mike had left the premises. He phoned every place his father might go without any luck. Finally he concluded Mike had decided to avoid him. He must find someone to hunt his dad down and change his mind—or stay in Tennessee. He called a couple of buddies, hoping they could persuade their fathers to talk to Mike. They were conveniently busy elsewhere. Jack learned he'd quickly become out of sight and out of mind. Worse than that, he was out of style. He had to find a way to go home—fast.

Dan followed Jack to the motel and presented him with an ultimatum. "You have two choices, Jack. Either you can pack your bags and hightail it out to the trailer, or pack your bags and go home with a pink slip."

Jack became furious. "Who do you think you are? You work for me, not the other way around," he ranted, but Dan couldn't be shifted.

"Actually, I work for your father, and so do you. As of this moment, you also work under me, and if I say the word, you're fired."

Red-faced fury turned instantly to chalk-white shock. For speechless minutes, Jack stared at Dan before he gave in. "All right," he muttered with obvious distain. "But the second the crew arrives, I'm moving into the motel until I go home."

Dan set him straight right away. "Sorry, it doesn't work like that." Dan watched Jack deflate. "Even after we start construction, your presence out there will still be necessary for the duration."

Jack tried every argument he could imagine, and a couple of extras, but Dan was destined to succeed. Nightfall found Jack unpacking in the little silver trailer.

Anger kept Jack from sleeping the entire night. The weather didn't help. He lay awake fuming as he listened to rain hitting the top of the metal structure. He tried his cell phone several times, but couldn't make contact with anyplace further than Norris. What a mess. How could his parents do that to him? He still couldn't believe his mother had gone along with that harebrained idea! All through the night he wrestled with his ricocheting emotions.

That's probably why he fell asleep about the same time the locals were waking up. Since some were up sooner than others, Jack's early morning visitor came and went without a single witness to the small act of uncorking a tank supplying Jack's trailer with running water.

The first clue of any wrongdoing came after Dan called and woke Jack to tell him he would be out in an hour. Jack dragged himself out of bed and headed for the shower, thinking a little water would help open his eyes. A little water was just what he got before it dribbled and quit altogether.

Unfortunately, Jack had always been really bad at reading clues, at least that kind. He dried off, blaming everyone under the sun for his predicament, and while he waited, he paced the five feet of trailer space and ranted some more. His colorful language had turned the air blue by the time Dan pulled into the tiny parking area. Jack stormed to the door immediately.

"Why did you stick me out here in this God forsaken place with no water?" He thundered his query the minute Dan opened his truck door. "No food, no water, no phone. It's inhuman to ask a person to live like this."

Dan stared at him for a moment before he replied. "Most of the people who live in this area live exactly like this. You had plenty of water when I left last night." Dan paused, a thoughtful look spreading over his face. "I'd say you had a visitor."

Jack didn't understand, but he followed Dan around the trailer anyway. Water dripping from the empty tank and the stopper lying on the soaking wet ground supplied ample evidence that someone had been up to mischief, and that Jack had slept right through the whole thing.

"Why would anyone want to do that?" Jack asked, obviously puzzled by the meaningless act of vandalism. Dan gave him a look that said he thought Jack was dumber than a box of rocks.

"I told you we were having this kind of trouble." Dan

emphasized the word *told*. "That's the reason you're here. We can't let this continue. Now we'll have to hire someone to come out and refill the water tank. Each time we have one of these incidents, it will slow down the operation and increase cost. I tried to tell you last night. We have to find out who's doing this and put them behind bars before we sustain real damage."

For the first time since his exile from Indianapolis, Jack stopped to ponder what Dan asked of him. He discovered he felt needed. Jack hadn't attended four years of college to prepare for detective work, but knowing he could do something that would make a difference felt surprisingly good. He would put his mind to work for the first time in a long time and prove to his father, and Dan, that he was more than just a piece of fluff.

Once he made up his mind to be helpful, he started planning. Being a pretty smart guy, Jack had earned good grades all through school and knew he could have done better if he'd put forth some effort. He had all the confidence in the world that he would have this intruder caught and out of their hair in no time. After that, Dad would welcome him home.

But he became frustrated in his venture from the start. Jack sat up all night two nights in a row and nothing happened. No one came around and no one tampered with anything. Having turned into a night owl during his last few years as a playboy became an asset when stalking night predators. Sleeping most of the day wasn't a hardship when the boring hours held nothing of interest. After two peaceful, starry, moonlit nights, he came to the conclusion that the perpetrator had decided to stop on his own, probably because of Jack's presence at the site. He joyfully resolved to go into town the following day and call his father. Determined to give Mike the good report as soon as possible, he believed this would be his ticket home.

Although the lobby of the motel where Dan had set up temporary headquarters sported a pay phone, Jack chose the mom and pop general store in Andersonville where, he'd been told, the owner also had a pay phone. He'd just as soon Dan didn't know he aimed to call his dad. He'd gained a gram of respect for the old geezer, and going behind his back didn't feel right. Jack nevertheless remained determined to leave this rural nightmare and return to the city.

As Jack stood in the back of the one-room store waiting for his connection, a small woman walked in. He estimated her height at five feet, three inches. He immediately noticed her sandy blonde hair, blue eyes, and fashion model thinness. That's where any resemblance to fashion ended. She wore a pair of baggy overalls, an old checked, oversized, work shirt, and gumboots. An ancient, wide-brimmed, felt hat was crammed on top of her head, and she carried a cloth bag. Slowly, but purposefully, she walked toward the counter. With each step, the room became more silent. He saw two women step away from the center aisle. The lady clerk seemed to shrink under the woman's solemn gaze.

The little hillbilly didn't say a word, just placed her bag carefully on the counter and waited for…something. Jack became intrigued and so caught up in the mini drama that he almost missed the hello from his father's secretary.

He turned away and applied himself to negotiating a conversation with Mike. By the time he failed and hung up, the woman had gone. But as he started to leave, he became aware of snippets of conversations around him.

"…surprised she wasn't carrying her shotgun. She usually is."

"I've never seen her wear anything but those old clothes of her father's…"

"…can't understand why she didn't kill him sooner, the way he treated her."

"I don't know why she lets that old Haber Judd follow her around…"

Very odd, very interesting, Jack mused, realizing he'd stumbled onto a puzzle, and he couldn't stand an unsolved puzzle.

At that moment, he realized the absent woman was the one he saw the other day when he turned on the wrong road. Now that he thought about it, there'd been an old black man working in the garden spot, too.

What had that one lady said? That she'd killed a man? He would be keeping his distance from that one, for reasons other than he couldn't tell her female gender by looking. He left the store harboring a great deal of disappointment due to the lack of a conversation with Mike. He immediately put the strange woman out of his mind.

* * * *

Ann Mason walked steadily back in the direction of her old flatbed truck and slid onto the seat behind the wheel. Coming to the store always proved difficult. She knew the rest of the customers would be whispering behind her back before she walked out the door. She didn't know what they said, but judging by the way they scurried out of her path, the gossip couldn't be anything good. Well, let them. She didn't need them. Ann didn't need anybody. She never had anyone except Haber Judd and Peanut anyhow.

She half expected Deke Hindricks, the sheriff of Anderson County, to materialize today for the purpose of harassing her, but he hadn't shown up. His absence seemed unusual because he knew her schedule almost as well as she did. You'd think after five years he'd give the whole business a rest, but he always hung around, obviously waiting for an opportunity to catch her out. He'd have a long wait. Ann was a careful woman. She touched the shotgun in its holder over the seat. Remembering she had a protective device on hand gave her comfort.

Haber Judd slid his tall, work-hardened body onto the other side of the worn bench seat. She noted his old overalls and flannel shirt were as clean as his kinky, salt-and-pepper hair. His lined, leathery, black face and coal black eyes were solemn. Her dog, Peanut, occupied the space between the two humans. She patted his head, started the engine, and drove away.

Her companion and only human friend, Haber Judd, taught her how to drive after Red died. That ability opened a whole new world for her. She could do a great many things she would never have been able to do without transportation. At least, she could do them easier and in greater volume than she had ever dreamed possible.

Now, Ann could deliver her eggs without pulling them to Andersonville in her wagon. Now, once a year, she could load her whittled figures in the Ford and drive into Knoxville to a gift shop that would buy all she could turn out. Now, she could sell, directly from the bed of her truck, all the vegetables she could harvest. Now, she could deliver the wood she and Haber Judd supplied for vacationers who willingly paid someone else to do the cutting. Life seemed good.

Or at least it would if people would leave her alone to do her work. Since strangers started building resorts and vacation homes in the lake area, she had someone coming around several times a year trying to buy her property.

A long time ago, before she was born, her great-grandfather, Woodrow Carter, owned four hundred acres of this prime Tennessee land. But the Tennessee Valley Authority built Norris Dam in 1936 and now most of that land lay under water.

Woody had been elderly and uneducated. They easily bamboozled him out of the lakefront part of the property, leaving him with only the ten acres the house sat on for her grandfather Jedidiah's inheritance. Jed Carter had, in his turn, passed the modest property to his only child, Ann's mother, Mary Sue Carter Randall. When she died, the land and house passed to Ann's father, Jessie Randall.

The land belonged to her now, but the achievement took a long time. When her disgraceful father forced her into marriage with Redford Mason, he made Red his heir. As a result, when Jessie died, Red inherited Ann's legacy. When Red died, as his wife, the land became hers. At last the property rested with its rightful owner.

Now people were trying to take that land, too. Ann had no intention of selling, ever. She'd lived there all her life. She wouldn't know how to live anywhere else, but she didn't know how to make them leave her alone.

Before Norris Lake became so popular, she barely eked out a living. Now that money proved more readily available, beating off people who wanted her land became the problem. Even though the property didn't set on the shoreline of the lake, the docks were nearby, making the location desirable.

The firm that bought the land, which butted up against her back boundary, had become the most persistent of all the pursuers. They had obtained the twenty acres that stretched from her property down by the lake. She heard they wanted hers because it would give them frontage on two roads. They weren't too crazy about having her eyesore, as they'd put it, in their backyard, either.

One of their men had even tried to court her. He sent flowers and asked her out to dinner and a movie. He seemed surprised, even shocked, when she turned him down. She smiled at the memory of his flabbergasted expression. He thought she would jump at the chance to go out with a fine-looking man like him. He took one look at her and saw a poor, deprived, love starved widow who would be so flattered by his invitation that she would be putty in his hands. If he had run a check on her background, he would've known better. No man could draw her interest, fine looking or otherwise. The two males she had in her life now were the only ones she wanted.

Chapter 2

Ann pulled her old Ford truck into the lane that ended beside her house and killed the engine. She sat for a moment, trying to see her place through the eyes of others. Her cabin sat on a little rise, giving it a humble sort of majestic pretense. The structures were old, but she saved enough money to buy white Exterior Latex and spent a couple of weeks painting the house and all the outbuildings. The drive was gravel, but neatly contained, and no trash littered the yard. Ann mowed and trimmed often, and she thought the flowers she planted made everything look nice. Of course, her place didn't have the opulence of the beautiful homes over on the lake, but she took pride in her accomplishment. The entire homestead had greatly improved over the way it looked when Red and her dad were in control.

She, the dog, and Haber Judd clambered out of the truck. Peanut followed Ann to the back where she had deposited the sack of groceries she traded eggs for at the store. Ann bent down and shared an affectionate cuddle with her faithful dog. Peanut created the only outlet allowed for her more tender emotions, and she lavished all of them on him.

As Ann poured out her passion on her four-legged friend, she pondered an easier life in which one might relax and forget about the past. In this better life, making enough money to live on one week at a time constituted the only problem she knew. Ann envisioned an existence where neighbors wouldn't whisper as she walked by and officers of the law loitered somewhere else. She craved a carefree life without the masses constantly exploring ways to steal her home. If only the rest of the world go away and leave her alone.

Ann turned with the sack clutched in her arms and walked toward her cabin, telling herself there must be a way of making those dreams come true. Ann had always trusted God to take care of her, and He had. He still would. She just needed patience—and faith.

* * * *

The very next morning, Jack awoke to a new disaster. All the air had been let out of his tires. This new prank would make him late for his meeting with Dan and the architect, Andrew Collins, who flew in last night for the purpose of showing the two of them his up-to-the-minute designs. Mike had already approved the changes, and today Collins intended going over the last minute details before Dan started moving in work crews.

Jack became livid. Now he'd have to call Dan on the

new phone line installed yesterday and ask for assistance. He stomped back inside and picked up the phone. No dial tone. He jiggled the disconnect button with no results. Exasperated, he slammed out the door and tramped to the side of the trailer where new wires were supposed to connect him with the outside world. He stared in amazement at the neatly clipped lead-in wires. He tried his cell phone, but a low battery denied access.

Jack berated his lack of vigilance, but couldn't understand why anyone would want to place him in this predicament. Almost seven miles of country road separated him from Norris. He couldn't imagine walking that far. That's something one might do for exercise, but not for the useful purpose of traveling from one place to another. Eventually, he admitted there was nothing else to be done, and he started out on foot.

Jack walked the main road, hoping someone would pass by and give him a lift. Eventually that did happen, but not before he'd sworn revenge when he caught up with whoever had sabotaged his belongings. And he would catch the guilty party. The bastard had just made a major mistake. He'd made the conflict personal. Jack could be a regular pit bull when roused to anger, and he'd now reached that point.

He arrived in time for the last of the meeting, and because of his status as the boss's son, they rehashed the information he'd missed. Concentration proved difficult because of Jack's anger, but he managed, just barely. Afterward, Dan gave him a ride back to the trailer. Jack fumed all the way, silently making covert plans for the annihilation of the nasty piece of work who continued complicating his life.

Now for the first time, Jack really applied his mind to figuring out how this scoundrel could be apprehended. Before, he'd assumed he could watch and wait, and the person would fall into his hands. Anger became a great motivator. Now Jack focused on the best way to track down the worthless scum, and what he would do once he caught him.

As soon as his tires were aired up, Jack zoomed into Knoxville and traded his Jaguar in for a fully loaded Hummer. While he was at it, he bought a Yamaha dirt bike. He also invested in surveillance equipment and paid an expert to show him how to set up the stuff. By the time Jack arrived at the trailer, he was spoiling for a fight and ready to take on all comers.

He spent the rest of that day and all the next setting up his new equipment. After the telephone company replaced the damaged wires, Jack arranged booby traps around them, hoping the vandal would be tempted to try the same trick.

On the third day, he hopped on the new dirt bike and rode the twenty acres of land surrounding the trailer. He soon realized the site could be approached from almost any direction. He still didn't understand why anyone would sabotage this particular undertaking with so many more profitable buildings around the lake. All his intense contemplation aroused a brain capable of so much more than Jack had yet asked of it. Once awakened, ideas bombarded his mind.

The following morning, Jack rode the Yamaha into Norris for another meeting with Dan. The crew was due on Monday, and the two men agreed the problems should be resolved before the workers arrived. After they discussed Jack's dilemma and the progress he'd made, Jack decided he might as well go to the trading post in Andersonville and nose around. He hoped he could pick up a piece of helpful information.

The minute he arrived, his attention zeroed in on the old rattletrap truck just pulling up in front of the store. He immediately recognized the driver as the plain woman who'd generated all the gossip the last time he'd been here, the one who had killed someone.

She'd just climbed out of the old vehicle when he pulled the bike up beside her. She glanced at him from the corner of her eye and turned away, stepping toward the store.

"Hello." Jack spoke with annoyance because the woman so blatantly ignored him. He wasn't used to that kind of treatment. He'd been sought out and coddled since the cradle by women from six to sixty, pretty and plain, rich and poor. Age, appearance, and situation made no difference. They all loved him, and why wouldn't they? Jack oozed good looks, he signified wealth and power, and he loved them right back. That's why he couldn't stand to let the snub pass. Pride insisted he win a greeting, even from this genderless individual.

But she didn't so much as acknowledge him. She continued toward the store with her loaded bag. Jack took two quick steps and placed himself in front of her.

"I said 'Hello,'" he growled. Two startled blue eyes flew to his face. Two naturally pink lips parted in surprise.

Ann looked up, way up, into the face of a very large, belligerent man, a very frightening man. He wasn't a stranger, though. She knew he lived in the trailer located on the property behind hers. Knowing he was her neighbor didn't help. She felt herself tremble and tried hard to hide the quiver. Life had taught her that showing an adversary your weaknesses created danger, the difference between winning and losing, possibly the difference between living and dying.

"Please move."

She murmured so low he could hardly hear. But Jack couldn't move. His gaze had become locked with sky blue eyes, the purest blue he could ever remember seeing. They were framed by long, coal black lashes that didn't match the wildly curling, sandy blonde hair on her head. Mesmerized as he was, he slowly became aware of the smooth, creamy skin surrounding those orbs. He pulled his attention from her fascinating eyes to drift lower, registering a pert little nose sitting right above bow tie lips that made his mouth water.

Jack's gaze automatically dropped lower. Old overalls and gumboots! Boy, he must be in bad shape, having lustful thoughts about one of the local yokels. He couldn't race back to the city fast enough.

Frightened by his sheer size, Ann didn't notice the utter gorgeousness of the man. She remained unimpressed by tall, dark and handsome anyway. Red possessed a handsome outer shell, but when his fists started flying, his good looks didn't make him any more appealing. Size and strength were the only considerations when flesh hit flesh.

Ann reluctantly took a step back. At the same time, Jack heard a menacing growl and saw a huge black dog slowly advancing toward him. The mongrel came an inch at a time, but to Jack he seemed to be running at Olympic speed.

"Sorry." Jack backpedaled as he took note of the gleaming fangs exposed by an impressive snarl. "I didn't mean any harm. Call him off. Please!" That last word came out sounding a little desperate, which was fine with Jack, because he felt a lot desperate. In his fertile imagination, that extremely large dog looked like a mountain by the time she finally stopped the beast three feet from his throat.

"Sit." She spoke the one word in the sweetest sounding voice he'd ever heard, and once again he became mesmerized. He stood waiting for her to speak again, but her melodious tone wasn't the one he heard next.

"Mister, Ah believe the Mam asked ya ta move so's she kin pass." The new voice sounded like rusty nails rattling around in a tin bucket. Jack turned toward the speaker and saw an old black man standing three feet away staring daggers at him.

"Problem?" Another voice came from his other side, and Jack spun around to confront the new threat. The man who spoke last proved to be help instead of hindrance. He stood about six and a half feet tall, had muscles on top of muscles, and he wore a gun—and a badge.

"Hello." The lawman nodded toward the mysterious woman whose path Jack blocked. "Haber Judd." He aimed that salute at the old black man. "I'm Deke Hendricks, and you must be new in town?" He directed that question to Jack.

"Jackson Barrister," he introduced himself. "And yes, I've only been in the area for a short time. My family owns the property on Lakeview Lane where we plan on building a resort." Jack gave the information reluctantly because he knew eventually he'd have to anyway, but he didn't like being questioned about his own business. He also knew, however, the value of good relations with the local community, especially the police.

"I know the place," the officer stated. "That's the property that backs up against yours, Ann."

Ann. Her name was Ann. It suits her, Jack thought. But why did he care?

"We're neighbors?" he asked the baffling young woman who still shied away from him.

"So it would seem," she answered in that sweetly melodic angel-voice before she turned and faced the big man with the gun. "Deke, haven't seen you in more than a month. I thought maybe you decided to leave me alone and let me live in peace. I guess that's too much to expect from a man who thinks I'm responsible for him losing his drinking buddy, huh?" Deke puffed up like a balloon and deflated just as quickly.

"Red was not my buddy," he stated with a great sigh of resignation as he stepped between her and Jack. "I've tried to tell you, just because we were in the same class at school didn't make us friends. And just because we had a drink together the night he died didn't make us drinking partners. You have to give up on this idea that I'm out to nail you." Deke emitted another great sigh. He could tell he wasn't making any headway, so he might as well back off. He stepped out of Ann's way, and she sidled by him like she might put her foot in something stinky.

Jack kept an eye on her as she slid past the man named Deke. The grace of her movements became apparent in spite of the shoddy fitting clothes. Though surprised at his interest, Jack couldn't force his eyes away. He stared until she disappeared inside the door of the trading post. As he battled the weird urges she produced in him, Jack realized Sheriff Hendricks was watching him watch her.

"You might as well shake off any notions in that direction, Son," Deke ordered, even though the shorter man looked about Jack's age. "She's a man-hater, trained, not born. Had a real mean husband, up 'til he died about five years ago. The sidewinder deserved the shotgun blast that killed him, no doubt, but his death didn't make that little gal's life any easier, except she's not walking around black and blue anymore."

"Did she shoot him?" The words just popped out of Jack's mouth. He hadn't intended asking any questions about the hick woman, but the gossip he overheard here the last time he came made him curious. Without thinking, another inappropriate question popped out. "Why does she dress like that?" His distaste must have been revealed by the tenor of his voice because the lawman turned his head and looked directly at him. Jack knew he'd been less than tactful by the way Deke stared him down.

"You wear what you have, and what she has is her daddy's old clothes," he told Jack. "That girl's more concerned with putting food on the table than she is with putting garments on her body. She'd buy dog chow before she'd buy a new shirt for herself." He paused for a second before answering Jack's first question. "Most people believe she shot the bastard. Some think the gun fired accidentally while he was loading it, because of all the shells scattered around on the floor. There's no way to be sure since she's not saying one way or the other."

"What did the investigators say?" Jack asked, feeling somewhat braver about his nosiness.

Deke shrugged. "The coroner ruled the death accidental. He may have been swayed by the fact that Ann had been beaten almost to death. A month passed before she started looking human again. At the time, investigators concluded Red meant to finish her off with the shotgun, but was so drunk he shot himself instead. She was never arrested, let alone tried or convicted. As far as I'm concerned, that makes her innocent."

Deke put a finger against the brim of his hat as a goodbye gesture and walked away. Jack's head whirled with unanswered questions. How could the police have determined that Red intended to shoot Ann? The man obviously liked using his fists, so why not continue beating on her? But there was no accounting for the way a drunkard would act. Jack had witnessed some pretty bizarre exploits pulled off by people under the influence.

Still trying to make sense of the puzzle he'd just discovered, he walked into the store. Silence met his ears. Jack looked around, observing the townsfolk huddled in various corners. Ann stood at the counter, back straight, head held high. She didn't look one way or the other as she waited for the clerk to finish with her business.

It must take a lot of courage to ignore such deliberate snubs, Jack thought. He found he admired her strength of character. He walked boldly to the counter and stood beside her.

"So we're neighbors?" he asked in a neighborly way. He wanted her and everyone else in the store to see she didn't scare him, that he considered her just an average Jo...sephine.

"So it would seem," she replied, tongue in cheek, fully aware they'd said these words outside a few minutes ago. She didn't bother looking at him, and Jack realized she had no intention of continuing the conversation.

"I'm having a little trouble out at my place," he stated, and marveled that he actually called that tin box his place. "Do you know of any reason someone would want to create a mountain of havoc in my life?" She flinched. He might have missed the microscopic recoil if his eyes hadn't been glued to her face. Though he knew staring was rude, Jack couldn't stop gaping at her. Looking for scars, he persuaded himself.

"No, I wouldn't know anything about that," she mumbled.

Jack detected an uncertainty in her voice that seemed at variance with the bravery she displayed only moments ago, but it seemed right in tune with the flinch. All those thoughts flew out of his mind a second later when she turned those sky blue eyes on him. "If I hear of anything, I'll let you know."

The most peculiar sensations he'd ever experienced swamped Jack. He felt winded and a little too warm. His mouth became dry. He had an almost irresistible urge to move closer.

Ann was scared spitless. She mentally wrung her hands and worried that he might learn something regarding her secrets. All she wanted was to leave, but he gazed at her in a way that paralyzed her legs. Warmth crept through her body. She needed to move, but the man's eyes held her in place like a doe caught in the lights of an oncoming car.

Jack stayed motionless, shocked by his feelings and his actions. He stood staring like a lovesick first-grader, making a fool of himself. He needed distance. With effort, he forced his head to nod goodbye and walked away with as much dignity as he could muster.

Released from the power of Jack's stare, Ann finished her business with Mary Jane, the store clerk, before she also left. Beneath the fear of discovery blossomed a foreign sensation, something new and different. She would have to be very careful around this man. He just might be more trouble than she could handle. Ann peeked out the door first, and exited when she had established he was gone.

* * * *

The second time Jack rode around his family's land, he stopped when he came to the back boundary where a tiny creek meandered its way between his and Ann's properties. He could barely see a roof through the trees, and thought it must be the woman's house. He waded across the shallow stream of water and edged his way closer to the mystifying creature's home.

In his mind, Jack visualized what he'd seen that first day when he made a wrong turn and drove past her house. He saw again the neatly kept cabin settled on a knoll among the majestic Tennessee Mountains. The azure sky formed a beautiful background for the weird woman in overalls and gumboots who wielded a garden rake. She toiled beside a black man working the earth with a shovel.

Jack found it difficult to associate that scene with the picture of creamy skin and sky blue eyes he'd carried with him since their meeting at the store. The image stayed in his mind all day and followed him into his dreams at night. He couldn't escape from the vision, and he didn't understand why. His reactions were perplexing.

Maybe coming onto her property wasn't such a good idea, Jack thought, as he moved close enough to see the house through the trees. He spotted the old man breaking up clods of dirt with a shovel, but he couldn't make out anything or anyone else. Jack didn't want to see the woman again anyway. He had no interest in her. She had just become a puzzle, and Jack couldn't stand unsolved puzzles.

He'd turned, with every intention of leaving, when he heard a sound like a twig snapping, and a low, throaty growl. Jack looked over his shoulder and saw the big dog he remembered from outside the store in Andersonville. The animal crouched low, the fur on the back of his neck stood straight up. His mouth drew back in a snarl and long, sharp fangs were clearly visible. Jack feared he had stepped into trouble.

"Nice doggie," Jack choked out. He knew better than to move. He couldn't have anyway, since his legs were locked with dread. "Nice doggie," he muttered as the carnivorous canine took a step in his direction.

Relief came in the form of the badly-dressed young woman emerging from behind a bush and placing her hand on the dog's collar. But his relief wavered when Jack realized she had a shotgun resting over her arm. Suddenly the story of the death of her husband flooded his mind, and her dog seemed the least of his worries.

"Hi," he croaked lamely.

"What are you doing here?" she returned without preamble.

That was a darned good question; one he didn't know how to answer. He knew she intended to wait until he came up with a realistic explanation, so he racked his brain for an acceptable excuse. "I just thought I'd pay a neighborly visit."

He finally coughed up an answer and felt quite proud of the plausible reason for his presence on her land.

"I want you to leave now, or I'll release Peanut," she threatened. Ann knew he hadn't come by for a visit. Everyone avoided her like the plague, which made her even more astonished at his reaction to her command.

"Peanut?" Jack had the nerve to sputter. "That big brute of a dog is named Peanut?" In spite of his precarious situation, his lips twitched with the effort to keep from laughing out loud. For some reason, the fact that the dog was named Peanut made Jack less fearful of him. Come to think of it, the girl with the gun wasn't quite so threatening when you knew she'd named the monster dog Peanut. He couldn't repress the laughter any longer.

Ann grew confused and a bit offended by his reaction to her dog's name. She'd never looked at the label from anyone else's point of view. She supposed Peanut's name sounded funny when you considered how big he appeared and how mean he sometimes acted. She gazed at the man who stood grinning at her—and smiled.

Jack instantly became enchanted. That smile transformed the little hillbilly's intriguing face to downright pretty. Whoa, buddy! Where had that impression come from? The thought sobered him fast, and his grin disappeared.

"All right, I'm out of here," he muttered, turning to leave. His quick departure had more to do with the outlandish ideas popping into his head than with the dog—or the shotgun.

Ann felt relieved, of course she did. So why the let down reaction? She didn't want a strange man around here. Besides, she now knew he was one of those people who were always trying to buy her land. She rejoiced because he had left so easily.

He sure was pretty, though. And he made her feel funny, different from anything she'd experienced in all her twenty-three years. Identifying these emotions proved difficult, even for her private peace of mind. Ann felt flustered, unable to think straight when he came near. She could have been excused for believing a herd of butterflies had taken flight in her belly. When he smiled, she became young again. She couldn't remember the last time she felt so frivolous and carefree, and she liked the sensation.

Ann returned home in time to start supper. Cooking had always been her job, and she excelled at it. She planned fried chicken for their evening meal, and had already prepared the meat for the skillet. All she had left to do was fry the chicken, peel and mash potatoes, put a jar of the peas she canned last fall on to heat, and make cream gravy.

While she dealt with their supper, Haber Judd fed and watered the animals and locked everything down for the night. When that was done, he set off to wash up in the barn he called home. After they ate, he helped her do the dishes. Then they sat down, her in the old rocker and him on the floor, while Ann read from her mother's tattered Bible. They both thought reading the Holy Word was the perfect ending for the day.

As Ann read, peace settled over her. The cares of the day shrank into manageable drops. They slid into a puddle of worries that she could leave on the floor until she rose from her bed the next morning and picked them up again. Those moments with Mother's Bible saw her through the bad days when she'd been abused almost beyond endurance. The peacefulness she garnered from reading the Word would see her through again.

When she slipped into bed, she fell asleep at once and dreamed of a tall man with thick brown hair and eyes so dark they looked black. He sported wide shoulders, narrow hips, and a long, lean body that looked strong and capable—a very handsome man.

In her dream, he drifted toward her, holding out a hand, but she backed away, afraid to trust the male of the species, and he slowly faded into a mist. She ran after him calling his name. Suddenly, out of the mist, Red materialized in front of her. Ann tried to stop, but her momentum carried her toward him. She struggled to prevent the forward motion, but continued on, moving closer and closer to certain doom. He pulled back a fist, and fear overwhelmed her until she cried out. Helplessly, she watched his club-like fist come at her face. She struggled harder...

Ann woke from the nightmare tossing and turning, bathed in sweat and shaking all over. Peanut had come when he heard her cries of distress and rested his great head on the bed beside her. She patted Grandma's quilt with a shaking hand, inviting him up. Coming out of the delusion and back to reality proved grueling. Fear still controlled her emotions as she sat in the dark with her dog, wide-eyed and trembling.

Ann knew from past experience that falling asleep again would be impossible, so she didn't try. She arose, made her bed, washed, and dressed. She set out fresh food and water for Peanut, made coffee and toast for herself, and took a chair at the table, attempting to blot out the visions of horror.

But no matter how hard she tried, she couldn't dismiss the dream because this time one thing had been different. The man named Jack had been part of this nightmare. He'd been reaching out to her. Could that difference mean something?

It probably meant that if she was stupid enough to trust the man, she could expect flying fists from him, too. No need to worry about that happening. She knew better. She wouldn't let herself become involved with a member of the opposite sex. Haber Judd and Peanut were the only males she would allow in her life.

Chapter 3

It was not quite three in the morning when Ann stepped out the back door of her cabin. The sky remained dark, but moonlight bathed the tops of the trees and buildings, turning them silver. She loved this time of day. The wee hours of the morning were so still and calm and peaceful. She felt like the only human being in the world. She felt safe.

In a few minutes, birds would wake up and the silence would be shattered with their singing. Almost immediately, the sky would begin to lighten, the rest of the world would awake, and life would speed up. Everything would go on as it usually did. She treasured these islands of peace before the bustle of everyday living hit.

But this morning would be different. This morning Ann had a mission. She intended making another attempt at discouraging Barrister Construction from settling in and building a resort practically in her backyard. She'd seen the changes that came with this kind of progress. Trash left by holiday makers took the place of mountain beauty. Streams became more and more polluted, killing more and more fish. The animals retreated deeper into forests for their own protection.

That had become a personal concern for Ann. Many winters she and Haber Judd supplemented their meager supply of food by fishing and trapping. Rabbit, coon, and once in a while, a deer made the small amount of money earned in the summer months last a lot longer.

Even though Ann now had more cash than before, making ends meet became harder simply because of all the visitors in the area. Tourism caused rising prices on everything. Food from the grocery store cost almost three times as much as she had paid in the past. Gas for her truck and the mower and tractor, when it worked, often became unaffordable. Taxes skyrocketed. She must save anywhere she could just to hold onto her home.

That comprised only one of the reasons she continued with her vendetta. She believed in the importance of saving these twenty acres from becoming another playground for the wealthy. Besides spoiling the natural beauty of her homeland, this kind of progress threatened her very survival. She must succeed in her efforts to drive these builders away; to make the project so much trouble Barrister's would abandon their plans.

Even her paltry ten acres combined with their twenty wasn't half enough to support the local animal population. They would surely move on to greener, or less crowded, pas tures. As a direct result, her problems would multiply. She doubted anything she did would make a difference, but she must try.

She moved on across her land, thinking of the modest influences her few exploits had achieved to date. They didn't amount to much, and she was running out of ideas. Pulling off her stunts had been easier when no one lived in the trailer. Now she had to watch her step or risk ending up in jail. Wouldn't that be a laugh? She would have avoided going to prison for the murder of her husband only to end up in the slammer for vandalism. Oh, how the townsfolk would love it.

Well, she had no intention of obliging them. They all stood by without lifting a hand while Red beat her to a pulp. Even further back than that, when her own father left her black and blue, they turned a blind eye. She would stand on her own, and win, if it was the last thing she ever did.

Ann realized she wasn't being completely fair. Several times, people from the community—teachers, lawmen, even Mary Jane—the store clerk from the trading post—tried to persuade her to admit the men abused her. However, Jessie and Red told her regularly that if she talked about what they called "her punishment" she would die before anyone could rescue her. She believed them. So, even though she resented the fact that no one helped her out of the terrible situation, Ann knew they weren't really at fault. The only ones she could blame were her father, Red, and herself.

* * * *

Jack lay sound asleep when Ann approached the clearing where his trailer stood. But that didn't last long. One of the motion sensors he'd installed last week set off an alarm beside the bed. The warning sound beeped loud enough to wake him, but not loud enough to let the intruder know he'd been detected.

Jack rolled out of bed wide awake, adrenalin pumping through his veins. This was it! Someone had approached the yard. He jerked his pants on, then his shirt, but didn't take time to fasten either one. He jammed his feet into well-worn tennis shoes and cautiously opened the door.

The moon shown outside with more light than he had inside, so his eyes were well adjusted. He scanned the area in front and, seeing nothing there, he eased out the door and began creeping along beside the trailer.

He had rounded the corner and faced the back yard when he saw a movement. It was only a shadow, really, and very vague, but Jack thought he was about to catch his man. Then the shadow moved again, and he identified the shape and stealth as that of an animal.

He knew the minute it sensed his presence. The creature stopped, sniffed the air and bounded away. Jack's conclusion came from impression more than sight. He didn't actually see the animal sniff the air, he sensed the action. As Jack's nocturnal visitor turned and retreated into the woods, he noticed a slight movement beyond. Only a flicker, then it disappeared as well. Probably a mate, Jack decided.

He returned to the front door and stopped for a moment to admire the early morning tranquility. As he stood watching, moonlight began giving way to the distant, unseen sun. Slowly the light changed from the ghostly beauty of the nighttime illumination to the growing expectation of a bright new day. The panorama held a splendor beyond Jack's jaded memory.

Almost as if on cue, birdsong filled the air. He stood for several more minutes enjoying the dawning of another Tennessee day and then ambled inside to start his morning over by brushing his teeth and having breakfast.

* * * *

Ann's trust in Peanut once again proved justified. She'd been on the verge of stepping out of the forested protection when her dog stopped and sniffed the air. She stopped just as suddenly and watched to see what had alerted him.

When she saw Jack step into view, she backed into the shadows and paused only a moment to admire his bare chest gleaming in the Tennessee moonlight. After that tantalizing glimpse, she turned and quickly made her way back toward her own land. Whew! That was close! One more step forward and she would've been in plain sight. He would surely have seen her.

She quickened her pace. Her heart raced from the fear of being caught snooping around where she had no business. Surely her constricted breathing wasn't caused by excitement. She didn't want him to catch her; that was true enough. But a little voice inside her head tried to tell her she really did enjoy seeing that bare chest. *That is not possible*, she thought before she dismissed the voice.

Ann felt a towering relief when she entered her own house and threw off her old hat and coat. The temperature remained cool enough in the morning to merit extra clothing, but later in the day it usually warmed up considerably. She hoped it would. She and Haber Judd still faced a lot of work to finish preparing the garden for spring planting. With great determination, she pushed all thoughts of her early morning failure, and the sight of a half-naked Jack, out of her mind.

* * * *

A few hours later, a visitor interrupted Ann's and Haber Judd's labor. They were first alerted to an interloper's presence by a low growl issued from Peanut. Both the workers rose from their tasks to see Jack Barrister stepping out of the woods at the back of Ann's yard.

She instantly broke out in a sweat. Could he have seen her this morning? It was possible. No, surely he would have brought the police if he'd seen her. Maybe he just suspected. Maybe he intended fishing for information. She stiffened her spine in fearful expectation and waited.

Jack slowed to a standstill. Peanut crouched low and moved gradually toward him. When Jack stopped, Peanut stopped as well, but he stayed in a defensive position. Jack remained too far-off for Ann to read his expression. She didn't know if he felt anxious, but she knew Peanut looked pretty fearsome in his protective stance.

"Hey neighbor, could you call off your man-eater," Jack yelled, eyeing the deadly-looking dog with a good deal of trepidation.

"Peanut, come." Ann spoke the command quietly and the dog responded immediately by going back and sitting at her feet. Jack took that as an invitation and proceeded toward her until he was within three yards. He stopped there and once again eyed the dog beside Ann.

"That's a pretty good watch dog you have," he commented innocently enough, but the praise didn't remove Ann's fear that he came to level some sort of accusation.

"Yes, he's an excellent guard dog." She tried to eliminate the hint of nervousness from her voice. "I believe he would kill for me." There, if that didn't put the fear of God in him she would walk to the end of the garden and pick up her shotgun. That usually proved enough to discourage most men.

"I can see how loyal he is," Jack said and let his eyes shift down, ogling Peanut's feet. "Hum...big dog, big feet. They remind me of the tracks I found in my yard this morning." He brought his gaze back to hers. "That's the reason I stopped by. I think someone may be cutting across your land and coming onto mine in order to commit vandalism. Have you seen anybody?"

"No." Ann had started shaking by now. She tried controlling her apprehension by the same methods she used when Red came home after sitting in a bar half the night. When he dragged her out of bed to pound on her, Red meant to see her cower, see fear in her eyes. She learned lots of tricks for hiding her emotions. She used one of them now, turning her head and looking at her fellow laborer. "No, I haven't seen anyone, have you, Haber Judd?" The old man shook his head. Ann turned back to face her inquisitive neighbor and met his eyes bravely, displaying not one drop of fear.

Jack examined her intently. She couldn't know his thoughts were far from intruders and vandals. He remained snared in his fascination with Ann's blue eyes and creamy complexion. As he stared steadily at her, she became fidgety. She tried first one method of self control, then another. Nothing succeeded.

"We have to get back to work," she blurted.

Jack startled out of his contemplation. He turned red in the face as he became aware of his actions. What on earth had happened to him? The woman was a hick, a tomboy at best. He found nothing about her appealing. She wore overalls, for Pete's sake! Nevertheless, he acknowledged pulling his gaze from her face became a colossal undertaking. "Thanks anyway," he mumbled as he waved a neighborly hand and retreated back the way he'd come.

Ann breathed a sigh of relief. She wouldn't admit, even to herself, that a small part of her nervousness stemmed from the fact that Jack was the most gorgeous man she'd ever seen. A blue chambray shirt stretched across mile-wide shoulders, narrow hips and long legs were lovingly molded by new-looking Levis, and his dreamy full lips made her mouth go dry. His sable brown hair, disheveled by his trek through the woods, looked wildly sexy. His eyes reminded her of a calorie-laden, hot-fudge sundae.

But not even in her dreams would she let herself be attracted to him. She'd been down that road before. The first time she saw Red Mason, she almost swooned. He had been tall with brown curly hair and blue eyes that twinkled with good humor. His lean body was strong and exciting to look at, until she discovered how that strength could turn against her when the good humor fled with the first swallow of whiskey. She decided she didn't want anything more to do with Red after seeing him drunk one time, but that didn't stop her Daddy from making her marry the man.

Ann brought her concentration back to Jack's visit. She remembered the way he came around the trailer that morning. Now she realized he must have known someone trespassed on his property, but how? He obviously had some sort of detection apparatus working for him. She would figure out how he knew she had entered his space. Ann remained determined to continue with her objective, but she would have to be very careful.

* * * *

Jack's thoughts were miles from intruders and detection devices. He'd flown into a panic over the strange emotions he experienced when that woman came near. Many of them were familiar, like wanting to touch her and kiss her and take her to bed. Those weren't new, but they affected him so much stronger than they ever had before.

And mixed in with those old emotions were new ones, like protectiveness. That was new. And he felt tenderness. Jack found himself wanting to bring her flowers and read poetry for her. Where had that come from? He never had those impulses before. Once again he acknowledged he needed to go home. Fast!

By the time he reached the trailer, Jack felt desperate enough to phone the last person he would ever have expected to call for help. Gina Lambert. They didn't start their acquaintance under the best of circumstances and their brief affair had ended even worse, but after trying to elicit assistance from his so-called friends earlier, Jack figured he'd have better luck with Gina. He certainly hoped he would.

Gina didn't answer her phone when it rang, so he left a message. She didn't return his call right away. She let him stew for three hours before she contacted him. He explained his need for help in persuading his dad to reconsider his position and asked if she would mention his dilemma to her dad. Maybe a word from Mister Lambert would soften the old man.

"What's in it for me?" she asked bluntly.

He hadn't thought that far ahead. "What do you want?" he inquired, but he was very much afraid he knew the answer.

"You," she stated, going straight to the point. Silence filled the phone receiver for a full minute. She sat filing her nails. He sat sweating. Jack knew a corner when he'd painted himself into one, but what choice did he have? He had to get away from this woman...place, he meant place.

"All right," he finally answered, still not quite willing to admit his interest in Ann had him running scared.

Now Gina sat forward, all business. "I can't come right away. I'm tied up for the next two or three weeks," she calculated. "After that, I'll manage to have a crisis only you can solve. When your father sees how well we're getting along, convincing him you're needed at home should be easy."

He agreed to her plan, but when he hung up, instead of relief, he had a feeling of doom.

Okay, he had two or three weeks to apprehend the nocturnal doer. That should be enough time. He required some sleep if he intended staying up half the night. He now had an idea where to watch. That should make the task a lot easier. He spent the rest of the day concentrating the surveillance equipment on the area where he'd seen the animal this morning.

To his intense frustration, nothing happened. The crew started arriving and, with them, the heavy equipment. It became more crucial that he find the problem-maker now, before some of this expensive machinery fell victim to the vandal.

He checked the wooded spot where he'd seen movement the day before, but nothing appeared newly disturbed. He decided running to the store for the few personal items he needed to see him through the following weeks should be safe enough. The suspect surely wouldn't make a move during the day with the workers on hand.

He could've traveled a few more miles to Norris where there were many more stores to choose from, but for some unfathomable reason, he drove to the trading post in Andersonville. He told himself quite emphatically that his choice had nothing to do with Ann, or the fact that the variety store was the only place he'd ever seen her away from her cabin. After all, he kept going to great lengths in order to avoid her.

Jack wouldn't admit disappointment at not finding her in the village. He lingered at the store, talking with the few people who wandered in and out. He bought a soda and drank it. Then he bought a candy bar and ate it slowly. He struck up a conversation with Mary Jane, and eventually he asked the question burning in his mind.

"I couldn't help noticing the young woman who came in the last time I was here," he started innocently enough. "You know, the one in overalls and an old hat. Does she come in often?"

Mary Jane didn't mind this kind of conversation. In fact, she loved chatting about everything. She wasn't malicious, just gabby. "You're talking about Ann Mason," she stated with self-assurance. "She comes in once a week mostly. Later, when the vegetables are ready for harvest, she'll come in three or four times a week. She's a nice girl. She's had a hard life though, what with that daddy of hers, and then that worthless husband." She practically spat the last word out of her mouth like the taste had turned rotten.

"Bad one, was he?" Jack asked. He waited with ill-disguised impatience for her to give him the information he didn't know he wanted—or why he wanted it.

"He was a snake! He made that poor girl miserable. She came in the store to sell her eggs with black eyes and bruises and scrapes on her face. Now and again she seemed to walk wobbly. I shudder to think what was hidden under her clothing. I asked her more than once if she needed any help, but she always said no." Jack could tell the whole idea made her irate.

"Why? Why would she refuse help?" he asked, truly puzzled.

"I think Jessie conditioned her from childhood to take a beating as her due. That father of hers beat her mother as long as I knew her, which lasted a good long time, and she didn't lift a finger to stop him. I offered to help her, too, but she turned me down. Ann was only two when her mother died. I think she took Mom's place under her daddy's fists." By the time Mary Jane finished her tirade, she'd turned red in the face and started breathing hard from anger.

Jack envisioned her as a heaping source of information and decided to take advantage. "I heard she shot her husband." Lowering his voice and leaning forward in a conspiratorial way, he murmured, "What do you think?"

"Makes no difference what I think. He deserved what happened to him. Besides, no one proved a thing at the time.

She seemed in such bad shape we all believed her incapable of pulling a trigger. If she's guilty of shooting the rat, she served her time before he died. That's what I say."

Jack thought for a minute about the story she related and found he wanted more details. "You say she seemed in bad shape? How?" He'd heard rumors, but he sensed there was a whole lot more. He wanted to hear the rest of the story.

"The way I heard it, the police received a call from a passer-by who saw Ann resting in the open door of her house. He thought she looked strange, so he hollered at her. Curious when she didn't respond, he moved closer. He saw she lay stock-still and bloody. Being a bright guy, he figured she needed help, so right away he called 911. While he gave their location to the phone operator, he looked past Ann and discovered Red Mason on the floor, dead. When the police arrived, they found Ann unconscious at the end of a trail of blood where she had apparently dragged herself to the door. She was almost unrecognizable. Her swollen face looked like ground meat. Her entire body had started turning black and blue. She had a broken leg and one arm broken in two places. Two fingers were broken. Investigators were convinced he intended to inflict as much pain as he possibly could before he killed her. His blood alcohol level was sky high. They concluded he'd tried to load the gun in order to shoot Ann and shot himself instead. Works for me."

"I'm surprised she survived injuries so severe." Jack's words came with difficulty. His mind reeled from the vivid picture painted by Mary Jane. He tried to block the image of Ann's beautiful skin pummeled by a man's fists until she bled. He didn't want to visualize her sky blue eyes swollen shut and surrounded by black and purple bruising. Broken bones! When he thought of her agony, he could feel her pain in himself.

"She almost didn't," Mary Jane continued. "It was touch and go for two days. We all thought she would die. I guess the bully couldn't kill her spirit, no matter how hard he tried. But living and being well are two different notions. The poor little thing was in the hospital for two weeks. They operated on her twice. Once for internal bleeding and once to put a metal plate on the broken bone in her leg. The hospital released her as soon as they could because she didn't have insurance to pay the bill. Another four weeks passed before she could put any weight on her leg. Doctors gave her therapy instructions which Old Haber Judd made sure she did faithfully. Though he could barely move from his own injuries, he took care of Ann all by himself. He said he owed her his life, so nursing her became his job and his privilege. We helped where we were allowed, which didn't amount to much more than a plate of food once in a while. We learned real quick all the damage wasn't physical. She didn't trust anyone. Still doesn't."

"Did you say Haber Judd owed her his life?" Jack questioned the one item in all that information he hadn't heard anything about, not a single hint. He just assumed the old man came along after the mysterious death of Ann's husband.

"Yep," Mary Jane answered. "It's pretty common knowledge that Ann found him on the side of the road half dead and nursed him back to health. At least, she nursed him for two days before she ended up in the hospital herself. But he had two weeks of healing before she came home, so by that time he had mended enough to take care of her. Mind you, he was still plenty wounded, so they both had a rough time."

A customer came in, so Mary Jane sighed and trudged back to work, leaving Jack with a brain full of facts that didn't compute. Once again, he asked himself why Red would stop beating Ann when he so obviously liked hitting her. And how could someone that damaged retrieve the gun, load it, and shoot a man who was in the middle of beating her to death.

Hmm… unless he'd already passed out before she picked up the shotgun. No, he wouldn't go there, because if that scenario proved valid, Red's death would be murder, not self defense. Besides, surely the investigating officers would have checked into that possibility.

One other piece of the puzzle had been added to the growing pile. If Haber Judd lived on the premises, and thought so highly of Ann, why didn't he come to her rescue? Had he been so ill he couldn't move?

Baffled, Jack pushed those ramblings completely to the rear of his brain. He returned to the everyday job of selecting the items he'd come to purchase, and keeping an eye open for the woman who occupied way too much of his consciousness.

He fought to keep her out of his thoughts all the way out to her house. He didn't plan on going there, but nevertheless that's where he ended up. Jack pulled into her drive and started to open the door when he saw the monster dog creeping toward him. He quickly calculated a change of action. He closed the door, rolled the window up most of the way and honked the horn.

"Hello, Peanut," he said, trying to sound a lot friendlier than the animal looked. Peanut growled. "Nice doggie," Jack said weakly. He wasn't at all sure Peanut could be a nice doggie, but if the lie worked, he'd use it.

He sat in the vehicle for five more minutes and sounded the horn twice before Ann appeared from around the corner. If Jack had allowed himself to think about the situation, he could not have explained why he hadn't just driven away, but he didn't let himself think about it, not even once.

When reasonable judgment regarding Ann was required, his mind became a wasteland.

He watched as she stopped in surprise at the sight of his Hummer. She appeared dressed the same as usual, overalls, checked work shirt, gumboots and the old felt hat. Ann had the shotgun over her arm, and when she saw him, she gripped the stock tighter. He felt shocked and unexpectedly wounded that she would take that attitude toward him. Jack refused to analyze why the idea hurt.

Ann stood shaken, surprised, and filled with apprehension. Why had he come? Had he found something she'd left behind at the trailer? She didn't think so. And why did he look so good to her. She prided herself on having more sense than that. But sense didn't seem to be a factor as she drank in his rich brown hair and chocolate eyes. Ann was helpless to prevent her interest from drifting lower until she gazed upon his sexy mouth. She licked suddenly parched lips. Even with the distorted vision through the automobile window, he remained a sight to behold. With great effort, she shook herself out of the daze his total hunkiness had produced.

"What do you want?" she asked, forcing the irritation she should be feeling into her tone of voice.

He just smiled. Something about her made him want to smile. *Must be the hat.* It sure wasn't the gun. "I kinda hoped you would call off the dog," he answered, tongue in cheek.

She became so entranced, she felt compelled to move closer. As she watched his lips twitch and his eyes sparkle, she found herself wanting to smile in return. He had the strangest effect on her.

"Why would I do that?" she teased. Was she actually joking, flirting, with this man, a rich city man who in all probability wanted her property, a man she didn't even know? *But you feel like you know him*, her common sense whispered. *Shut up*, she told the deranged little voice.

"So, I can leave the truck?" he quipped, and this time he really smiled. The sight completely dazzled her. Never in her life had she been treated to such a mega-watt smile. Her small town existence hadn't prepared her for the likes of Jackson

Barrister when he turned on the charm. But life had conditioned her to be distrustful, and those two perspectives were warring with each other right then. In spite of the raging battle, Ann gave in to the glittering temptation.

"Peanut, come," she commanded softly and her pet responded immediately, going to Ann and sitting at her feet.

Jack opened the door of his truck cautiously and climbed out, showing respect for the dog who obviously adored his mistress. "He's very well trained. How old is he?" Jack asked that question, but what he really wanted to know was if Ann would let him kiss her, and what she would taste like if he did. And if she did let him, where would it lead?

Chapter 4

What on earth was wrong with him! He had to get a grip! But he couldn't stop staring at her mouth. Her lips were naked and naturally pink. They looked soft and sweet. Could anything look sweet? Her lips did. He wanted to find out. He wanted to kiss and taste and...

"He's six years old, and I've had him all his life," she answered, interrupting his lustful contemplation. "Someone put him in a sack and threw him out of a car when his eyes were barely opened. He was too young to eat in the regular way, so I fed him with an eye dropper. That's why I named him Peanut. He seemed that small at the time. I had no idea he would grow up to be so big and strong." All the time Ann told her tale, she stood mesmerized. She remained perfectly still and let Jack approach her, watching his sexy lips and graceful body until he drew too close to ignore.

"Stop right there," she said in a small, breathy voice that wouldn't have stopped a caterpillar. As she examined his exceptional good-looks, her heart shifted into overdrive. She peered way, way up and thought he must be over six feet tall. His shoulders looked so broad. Her eyes followed his well-muscled arm downward and she noticed his hands. They were big. Red's hands had been big, too. Big hands hurt. She came out of her self-imposed absorption to see how close he'd come and, in a flash, she felt afraid.

"It's okay." Jack tried to soothe her as her expression moved from one of interest, which he anticipated, to one of fear, which he did not. "I won't hurt you," he said, trying to undo the change that had come over her. Before he knew what she intended, he found himself on the business end of a shotgun in the control of a very nervous woman.

"I think it's time you state your business." Her voice had turned as cold as ice.

Jack knew when to cut his losses and run, so he moved away. "Just trying to be neighborly," he said, holding his hands in the air and backing toward his Hummer. He gave her another one of his killer smiles as he turned and opened the door. "I'm going, but can you tell me whatever happened to southern hospitality?" He tossed the query as he jumped in the truck, started the engine, and drove away.

Ann stood rooted to the spot for several minutes before she could force herself back to work. Why did she feel so let down because he'd gone? She should be glad. She didn't understand the see-sawing emotions that were playing havoc with her analytical abilities.

In all Ann's life she'd never experienced so strong an attraction to a member of the opposite sex. The new urges pursuing her were totally perplexing. Why did she want him to stay when she'd told him to go? Why did she long for his touch when she was afraid to have him touch her? The conflicting emotions made no sense.

No matter how hard she tried, she couldn't boot the man out of her head. Every time she forgot to concentrate on the job, thoughts of him flooded her brain. She would find herself staring into space until Haber Judd or Peanut gently reminded her she should be working. She would pull herself together for a while, until it happened again. She became desperate to rid her world of his disturbing presence.

Jack battled a bewilderment that equaled Ann's and then some. At last he admitted—to himself—that he had a yearning for that peculiar little hillbilly. The admission didn't help a bit with figuring out how to handle his unwelcome desires. As a rule, he dealt with sophisticated women who wanted the same perks from a relationship he did—good company, good sex, and goodbye.

At least, that's what he believed until the episode with Gina. That experience ended as an unpleasant eye-opener. He still had trouble seeing his behavior through his father's eyes, but he could now acknowledge the sour-tasting incident with Gina proved to be an example he'd needed for a long time.

His new-found modesty didn't help him resolve his problems regarding Ann. He didn't want to insult her. He wanted to make love with her. But he felt as good as certain that Ann wouldn't accept a casual affair. Where did that leave him?

* * * *

At three forty-five the next morning, Ann crept out of bed. She'd been awakened by dreams of a dark haired, dark eyed man who made her crave things she had no business wanting, things she'd never desired before. Things she'd only read about. Today, Ann intended to send him packing!

She dressed, ate a meager breakfast, loaded her shotgun, and called for Peanut. They stepped outside into the moonlight and, as she always did, Ann stopped to admire the majesty of her homeland. There was nothing in the world as beautiful as an early spring morning bathed in silvery Tennessee moonlight. She sighed, enjoying the silence and the sweet morning air. Next, possessed of a fierce determination to rid her life of his threat, she headed for Jack's trailer.

Ann practiced extreme caution as she approached the clearing where he lived. She checked the ground, bushes, and tree limbs as she moved along, making sure she didn't trigger a warning. When she visited here the last time, exposure came a little too close for comfort. She learned a lesson she didn't aim to ignore. She had no intention of letting him find her sabotaging his efforts to establish a bigger, better resort. Ann had intelligence and strength of mind; unfortunately, she didn't know beans about motion sensors.

The alarm beside Jack's head woke him abruptly from a beautiful dream starring Ann. She wore a slinky red dress covered with those shimmery things, and she had on fishnet stockings with a pair of the highest-heels he'd ever seen. Her sandy-colored curls looked different, long and piled high on her head in a sophisticated do. Her lips were painted red and she wore loads of blue eye-shadow on her lids. For some unknowable reason, he tried to wipe the make-up off. He remembered telling her she looked better without the goop.

At the sound of the alarm, he rolled out of bed silently and pulled on his jeans and tennis shoes. Shoving his arms into his shirt, he peeked out the window and, lo and behold, he spied the elusive perpetrator.

Ann stood about twenty feet away from the trailer pouring sugar into the gas tank of his bike. Suddenly the door flew open and Jack came roaring out toward her. The sight of him in a towering rage scared her half to death. She attempted to raise the shotgun for protection, but in her nervous state, she accidentally fired the weapon.

In the next half-second, two things happened. Well, actually, three. Jack stopped dead in his tracks at the loud sound of the shotgun discharge. The look of astonishment on his face at seeing Ann standing in his yard, holding a smoking shotgun, would have been priceless, but she didn't have time to enjoy the irony. The blast from the gun sent a load of buckshot whizzing by Jack, missing his left forearm by an inch, and hitting the propane tank located right behind the trailer. Before the horrified expression on his face had completely formed, an explosion rocked the earth around them and both Jack and

Ann were thrown backward onto the ground. A few pieces of aluminum flew high in the air and showered down on the surrounding area. Micro-seconds later, they were both staring toward Jack's trailer when the structure burst into flames.

A state of disbelief consumed Ann. She abhorred violence of any kind. To think she'd been the instigator of such unwarranted destruction defied imagination.

Jack turned to face her with a look of such total incredulity that it might have been funny if her mind hadn't been otherwise occupied. But it was.

"Peanut!" she cried as she scrambled up. "Peanut!" The cry became a shriek. She operated on one level. The only thing in the world that loved her might be injured...or dead.

"You're a crazy woman," Jack roared. "You just blew up my trailer, and you're worried about your stupid dog! I don't believe it!" Reaction set in. He grabbed her upper arms and began shaking her. "Crazy, crazy, crazy," he continued yelling.

From out of nowhere shot a bundle of raging fur and snarling teeth. Peanut flew through the air, hitting Jack in the chest, forcing him to let go of Ann, and knocking him to the ground. Operating on pure instinct, Jack threw up his arm to protect his face and the enraged animal latched onto it, sinking his fangs into the flesh. Jack let out a scream of pain.

"Peanut! Release him," Ann called frantically, but the command took a second to penetrate his canine brain. Finally Peanut let go and stepped back an inch or two, leaving Jack with a bloody arm. Ann didn't have to move closer in order to see Jack's wound. She jerked off her coat and the old checked shirt to reach the tee shirt she wore underneath. Ripping a wide strip from the bottom, leaving her midriff exposed, she started wrapping his arm tightly.

Jack was paralyzed with shock. He felt too much pain to notice that patch of white skin peeking from under the torn shirt. Really, he did! So why did his eyes stay glued to her middle.

The appearance of a still angry dog beside his face took his mind off Ann's tummy. Peanut showed his fangs again and Jack underwent a certain reluctance to discover the sting of having his nose ripped off by those impressive teeth.

"Ann," he muttered, barely making a sound, partly from shock and partly from fear of enraging her pet even more. Peanut inched closer, touching his nose to Jack's. "Ann, call him off." Fear gave his voice strength and she heard him this time.

"Peanut. Sit. Stay," she instructed the big man-eater and, to Jack's extreme relief, he obeyed.

"We need to move you over to my place," Ann said. As she gazed around at the mess she'd created, she tried to organize the chaos in her mind. They needed antiseptic for his wound, but they couldn't just leave the blazing trailer. She looked around for a source of water to combat the flames.

At first, Jack didn't understand the direction of her thoughts. At about the same time her purpose sank in, he realized she suffered from shock, too. He rose, intending to take hold of her arm. He meant only to move her away from the danger present in the aftermath of an explosion, but Peanut had other ideas. The minute Jack stepped toward his beloved mistress, the dog erupted into action, placing his body between the two of them, and threatening Jack with limb severance.

"Ann," he said as loud as he dared with that animal staring straight into his eyes, "Ann!" he repeated when she didn't respond. Jack feared he would be unable to give her the help she needed with Peanut in the way. Then the most amazing thing happened. Peanut turned away from Jack, and using his teeth, took hold of Ann's clothing, and pulled. She looked back at Peanut's firm tug and Jack could see the dazed expression on her face. "We're going for help. Come on," Jack shouted and turned toward his vehicle, filing that tantalizing piece of information about Peanut away for later examination. Evidently the dog possessed great intelligence and would do anything in defense of his mistress.

Ann continued having trouble with her thought processes, but she nodded at Jack's suggestion and followed him to his monster truck. He felt in his pocket for the keys, but they weren't there. He cursed his conscientiousness. How many nights had he forgotten to lock the truck door? Why couldn't tonight have been one of those nights? In frustration he grabbed the handle and pulled. The door swung open. Ha! It was tonight. Never in his life had he been so grateful for his own screw up. Now if he could only remember how to hot wire.

When the engine finally started, he persuaded Ann and Peanut into the vehicle. The dog suddenly became very co-operative. Jack supposed he somehow sensed they all needed help.

Jack drove to the nearest house, woke the owners, and begged the use of a telephone. Once he explained about the fire, he received all the help he needed.

The day turned into a long one. Fire trucks came. Para-medics came. Police came. The questions were endless. When Jack's wounds were dressed, both he and Ann assured authorities they were all right. They just wanted to clean up and rest. Finally Jack insisted they let him take Ann home. When they asked where he would be staying, Jack looked directly at Ann's dirty face and told everyone he'd be staying with her.

She didn't dare say a word. So far, he hadn't told anyone the truth about how the fire started. He allowed them to believe she'd been a guest at his dwelling. She could only wonder how they would interpret her presence at the trailer in the wee hours of the morning, but nothing could be done about that. She certainly couldn't explain what she'd really been doing there, could she?

Jack loaded his passengers into his automobile in preparation for the trip to Ann's house. He let Peanut crawl into the back and stuck Ann in front before he climbed into the driver's seat. He spent the entire ride with hot doggie breath heating his cheek after Peanut pushed his huge furry face between the two of them. The big brute kept reminding Jack that he could take his ear off with just one snap of his teeth.

The afternoon had become late by the time they reached Ann's house, and they discovered they hadn't yet dealt with all the questions. Haber Judd was angry. He'd started worrying about Ann as soon as he came up to the house for breakfast and found her gone.

In the five years he lived there, except for the time right after her husband died, she always had breakfast ready by sun up. He began looking for her immediately, knowing something must be wrong. He grew more agitated as his search proved fruitless. He made his way to Jack's place and saw all the commotion, but nobody could tell him where either Jack or Ann had gone. At last he found a man who'd seen them at a neighbor's house. In spite of the worry in his heart, he made himself do the chores he'd planned for the day. He knew that's what Ann would expect.

The minute Jack's truck pulled into the drive, he came running from behind the house. He moved to the passenger's side and opened the door before Ann could lift the handle. He offered his hand and when she stood before him, he searched every inch of her, looking for damage.

He viewed a different Ann than the one he usually saw. She appeared filthy and half dressed. Her remaining shirt was torn. She'd ended up with scrapes on her face and a bruise hardly noticeable under all the dirt. Her arm had a long scratch. He immediately glared at Jack.

"Whachue done ta her?" he bellowed and started around the hood of the Hummer with murder in his eyes. Jack knew when to retreat. He jumped back into the truck and locked the door.

"Haber Judd, I'm okay," Ann called. "My injuries are not his fault. He didn't do anything." The old black man stopped his pursuit and turned back.

"That a fact?" he asked, going to her and pointing at the spot on her arm, his eyes touching the wounds on her face. "How'd this git heah?" Before Ann could reply, Jack, who had opened the door and stepped out, answered for her.

"The truth is your wonderful friend visited my place to commit vandalism. She blew up my trailer, but she made a slight mistake. I came outside before it exploded." He spoke very derisively. Haber Judd heard the words, but the tone shot right over his head.

"Naw sir. The Mam wud'n do nothin' lack that." He jumped to his friend's defense. "She be a good soul." Jack didn't know it, but Haber Judd just paid Ann the highest compliment he knew.

She couldn't let her loyal buddy believe a lie though. She strictly adhered to truthfulness, so she'd have to bite the bullet and tell Haber Judd the whole story.

"Yes, what he says is true, Haber Judd," she told him, laying a hand on his arm and looking into his eyes. "I've been going over there for more than a month trying to run them off before they ruin even more of the land Grandfather once owned. If my plan had worked, I'd have no regrets, but it didn't. I guess I don't know enough about being mean to make them leave." She sighed. "I supposed it's just a matter of time before I'll be forced into selling my land to Barrister's, but don't worry, I'll find a new home for us."

"Now wait a minute," Jack squeaked. "No one's trying to take your land."

He so emphatically stated his case that Ann almost believed him. Almost. He might be convinced, but she didn't buy that bill of goods. She sighed again. The breathy exhale contained so much regret that Jack's heart skipped three beats. "Your company's been after my home for years. Now you finally have the means to take it."

She spoke in the saddest voice Jack could ever remember hearing.

The look on his face told Ann he didn't understand what she implied, so she explained her theory. "When you have me arrested for blowing up your trailer, I'll have to sell up for the money to pay the damages. I'm sure you'll be very reasonable and offer a fair settlement in exchange for my home."

Jack felt exceedingly insulted. "What kind of person do you think I am?" he huffed. "I've never given you any reason to think so badly of me. Why would you say such a thing?"

Ann tried judging from his tone and expression if he believed what he said. He certainly appeared sincere. Puzzlement furrowed her brow. "Do you think you're the first one coming around here, trying to become friendly before making me an oh, so generous offer for my place? I know you think I'm just an uneducated hick, but I can smell a con a mile away." She gave him a look that said she found him stupid for assuming she couldn't see through his smokescreen, then she turned to the old man. "Do you think you can put him up with you, Haber Judd, or should he stay in the hen house?"

"Ah kin find a spot for 'em if'n ya say so, Mam, but if'n 'e's gonna take yer place, why ya put'n 'em up?"

Haber Judd's voice filled with a fire she hadn't heard in a long time. Ann knew his protective instincts were roused. She knew what he was capable of when angered, so she figured she'd better calm him down a mite. "I'm the reason he has no place to stay," she said quietly. "And no matter what my reasons were, destroying his property was wrong." She smiled at him.

Though he didn't understand why, Jack felt jealous of the old fart for the attention and care Ann lavished on him.

"I'm tired now, I think I'll clean up and rest a bit before I cook supper," she announced, and turned toward the house.

"Wait just a minute. You can't make accusations like that against me and walk away!" Jack took a step forward only to find Haber Judd right in his face.

"Mister, Ah believe the Mam says she's gonna clean up 'n rest a spell. Ah'm a guessin' ya need ta be doin' the same thang."

The two men eyed each other. Jack didn't doubt for a minute he could take the old man, but he looked at the work hardened muscles and decided a tussle with him would hurt, a lot, so he nodded.

"All right, Mister Judd." Jack smiled, applying a dab of his famous charm to the tense situation. "Lead the way." Stepping aside, Jack motioned his host ahead.

"Ever one call me Haber Judd. Don't answer ta nothin' else," Haber Judd told Jack as he passed by. "One thang ya need ta know. If'n ya hurt the Mam, in any way, yer gonna have me ta deal with. Ya heah?"

The old gentleman made it clear he expected an answer, so Jack gave the only one he could under the circumstances. "Yes."

In the barn, Haber Judd showed Jack where to find soap, towels, and water for cleaning up, and he left him alone. He came back later with a stack of clean clothes and told Jack "the Mam" said he could use them since she'd burned all his. Jack thanked the old man and tried the bits and pieces on. They weren't too bad, a clean pair of jeans that fit pretty well, a checked work shirt a size too small, white socks, and a pair of boots that were too snug. Those he discarded, preferring his muddy tennis shoes.

Minutes later, Haber Judd returned to take him in for supper, and all at once Jack realized his backbone and his belly button had become inseparable. His hunger could have stemmed from the horrendous day he'd just endured. His appetite might have been whetted because he'd eaten only a sandwich for lunch and nothing the rest of the day. But Jack suspected the wonderful smell floating out the window of Ann's kitchen was the main reason his innards rolled and his mouth watered.

"Mmm...something smells good," Jack said as his stomach growled. He couldn't remember the last time he'd been so hungry. He could hardly wait to taste Ann's cooking.

He and Haber Judd walked through the door directly into a medium-sized, old-fashioned room with white paint on the walls and aged linoleum on the floor. Two yellow-curtained windows gave natural light, revealing an antique cabinet with old dishes behind a glass panel, and a rack for Ann's shotgun. Beneath one window sat an ancient, chipped porcelain sink with two mismatched facets. A round oak table stood in the center of the room loaded with bowls of mashed potatoes, Ann's home-canned corn, homemade biscuits, and a platter of fried fish—blue gill that Haber Judd caught earlier that day. Jack's mouth watered again, but he wasn't looking at the table.

Ann had just turned away from the stove. She'd washed her hair and left the tresses drying in ringlets around her head. Her face was rosy from the heat of the old wood stove that had sat in this kitchen since her great-grandfather built the house for his bride. A short nap had added a teeny sparkle in her sky blue eyes. And suddenly Jack knew he'd never seen a more beautiful woman in his life. He couldn't look away.

Ann didn't know why Jack stood staring at her, but his intent gaze made her feel uneasy. She raised a hand and touched her hair. Maybe the unruly curls were standing on end. His sure weren't. He was still the best looking thing she'd ever seen. She couldn't pry her eyes away. Suddenly, without warning, Jack sprang forward.

"You're hurt!" he exclaimed reaching a hand toward her face. Just that suddenly, Peanut pushed between them, snarling and showing his pearly whites again. Jack pulled his hand back and stepped away, but not too fast, lest the big monster took offense and showed him again how much those teeth could hurt.

"Peanut, it's okay," Ann told her faithful protector, and she rubbed his head as he settled beside her. The black fiend's tongue lolled out of his mouth and he closed his eyes in obvious pleasure.

Jack gritted his teeth with the knowledge that he'd loll with pleasure, too, if she rubbed him. "How bad are you hurt?" he asked. Paramedics had cleaned and bandaged his wounds at the home of the good neighbors who'd let him use their phone, but Ann didn't tell anyone about the wounds she had hidden beneath a layer of dirt. She looked surprised that he would even ask.

"I'm all right."

Her statement had the ring of truth, but Jack had the distinct impression she wouldn't tell him if she were dying. He turned to Haber Judd.

"Would she tell you if she hurt?" he asked the only person he knew she trusted.

That Jack had sense enough to see beyond Ann's bravado impressed Haber Judd. She'd fooled everyone for as long as he'd known her. Convinced them, and perhaps herself as well, that she didn't need anyone, that she was superwoman. Maybe this one could thaw out the frozen heart of the most important person in his life. So he laid his cards straight on the table.

"Naw sir," he answered Jack in his rusty nail voice, eliciting a gasp from Ann.

"Haber Judd!" she squawked. "I can't believe you said that!"

Jack laughed at her indignation. Evidently laughter came in short supply around the Mason household because everyone, even the dog, stared at Jack as if he'd lost his mind. That just made him laugh more. He recognized the uncontrolled laughter as a release from the day's crisis, and happiness did feel good, so he laughed harder.

Haber Judd's lips twitched. A twinkle started in his eyes. A belly laugh erupted from his mouth and joined Jack's. Ann took a little longer. She hadn't laughed much. But nature finally won out. She smiled, then grinned, and finally laughed—a tinkling, musical sound that reminded Jack of the wind chimes his Aunt Lillie had always loved. He stood spellbound.

In light of these new emotions, keeping up the cheerful façade became a chore, but Jack wanted the smile on Ann's face to remain intact, so he worked at his happy countenance. They were still in this jovial mood when they sat down for supper.

Jack would have dug right in, and in fact had started to do just that, when Haber Judd loudly cleared his throat. When Jack looked at him askance, he gave an infinitesimal shake of his head. Jack turned toward Ann and saw she had bowed her head to say grace. Embarrassed, he realized he hadn't even thought of giving thanks. He wasn't surprised that she prayed. She wore her faith like a robe, and it suited her.

The food tasted every bit as good as the smell led Jack to believe. He ate every bite with gusto and asked for seconds, a display of enjoyment that would flatter any cook's ego. Ann proved no exception. He even insisted on helping with the dishes.

After they finished cleaning up, Haber Judd fetched the Bible and placed it on Ann's rocker. She looked at the good book, and then at Jack's confusion. Finally she turned to the old man.

"I don't think this is something that would hold appeal for our guest, Haber Judd." Ann's murmur held a wealth of reluctance. "Perhaps we should skip tonight." Before her friend could answer, Jack put in his two cents worth.

"Don't change your routine on my account," he insisted. "Besides, I might like whatever you've planned. Why don't we try it and see." He sat down on the floor beside Haber Judd and waited expectantly.

Ann found herself in a quandary. She didn't want Haber Judd disappointed, but she hesitated to impose her Christian practices on an outsider, knowing they were unorthodox. On the other hand, she didn't know what his religious beliefs were. She might as well introduce him to hers. Why not? She picked up her mother's Bible and started reading.

Chapter 5

The minute she spoke, Jack became ensnared by her voice. Never before had anyone sounded so sweet and musical. He relaxed and, as he listened, peacefulness washed over him. Cares of the day fell away like leaves drifting down from an autumn tree. Her voice soothed like a caress upon a tortured soul, gentle and melodious. Healing. The words eased a burden he didn't know he carried. Jack felt at rest. He fell deeply asleep.

"I told you he wouldn't like this," Ann whispered to Haber Judd when she saw Jack's head slump forward, but Haber Judd just motioned her to continue. It didn't take a lot of persuading. This was one of her favorite times of the day.

When she reached the end of the chapter and finished for the night, Haber Judd woke Jack and they retired to the barn. The men didn't talk on the way out, and Jack's host stayed too busy hunting blankets and showing him how to make a bed out of a pile of straw for conversation beyond yes, no, and thank you. After they lay down for the night, Jack stretched and yawned.

"Can't remember when I've enjoyed an evening so much," he told Haber Judd as his eyes drifted shut. "I especially liked listening while Ann read. Her words and her voice soothed and calmed. Just what I needed after our dreadful day."

The old black man felt secretly elated by this confession. "Maybe you should tell her."

Ann locked the door and undressed for bed, feeling a lightness of heart that conflicted with the fear of losing her home. She felt too tired to mull over the inconsistency, and in less than five minutes had fallen asleep. But, in that short amount of time, she concluded that Jack stacked up as model-perfect, movie-star material. That deduction became a good foundation for her dreams.

Jack slept surprising well for being in a strange place on a really strange bed. He'd drifted off to mountain night-sounds and the smell of clean hay. In his sweet dreams, a fairy tale princess wore overalls and gumboots and carried a shotgun. She possessed the bluest eyes in fairytale land and when she laughed, she made music. He became her prince.

* * * *

The next morning, Jack roused instantly at a touch on his ear and knew exactly where he lay and who stood beside him. He became extremely distressed by waking up face to face, literally, with his nemesis. Peanut stood nose to nose with him. Jack instinctively froze.

Sweat beaded on his forehead and rolled into his hairline. The bite on his arm started throbbing, a reminder of Peanut's strength. Before he could call for Haber Judd, he received an even greater surprise. Peanut stuck out his tongue and licked him right on the mouth. Startled and wide-eyed, Jack waited to see if that had been an appetizer. That's when he noticed Peanut's wagging tail. Amazing. Jack slowly brought his hand up to the dog's face, expecting at any moment it would be snapped off, but the mutt licked that, too. Jack patted the big furry head and Peanut let him. How about that? Maybe he could feel safe around the creature now.

After a great start like that, he figured he couldn't expect much more, but he was wrong. He and Haber Judd washed up in water carried from the pump. Jack usually took a hot shower, but he felt clean and quite refreshed following the cold sponge bath. After they bathed and dressed, Jack helped Haber Judd with the pre-breakfast chores of feeding and watering the goat and chickens, then followed him inside.

Ann served a phenomenal breakfast of pork sausage, cream gravy, fresh eggs from her own chickens, toast from bread she baked two days ago, and coffee made from freshly ground beans. She said grace and they dug in. He made a pig of himself. After clean up, Haber Judd began his workday and Jack tackled the big issue.

"Okay, Ann," he commenced, "tell me why you think I'm after your home."

Amazement flooded Ann at his choice of conversational topic. Now that she knew why he kept coming around, she believed he would try avoiding the fact. His question surprised her. "Experience," she stated flatly. "That's what the others who came from Barrister's wanted."

Jack mulled that over for a moment. "Who were these others?"

Ann rolled her eyes. So he intended playing dumb. Okay, she'd play along. "Well," she began, "there's William Fowler. After him, Bill Dickerson, and John Harrison came last. I think he would've married me in the name of company progress. You should definitely give that man a raise."

Jack's mind labored to make sense of what she said. He didn't know anyone named William Fowler, but Bill Dickerson sounded familiar, and he definitely knew John Harrison. "I know the men. They do work for us, but I can't believe their actions were sanctioned by my father." Jack spoke as his brain processed her statement. "I'll look into your accusations. Okay?" Ann nodded her head warily before Jack continued. "Be assured that's not why I visited you. I came looking for the vandal."

Ann's head popped up at the reminder of her criminal actions, and the smile spreading over Jack's face surprised her again. That grin strongly affected her insides. They seemed to go haywire. Little explosions made her tremble and quake internally. Everything in her body jumped around, and her mouth seemed dry as a cotton ball. She licked her parched lips.

Jack saw that small pink tongue dart out and felt a jolt of reaction through his body. Had he ever been affected like this by the sight of a woman's tongue? If so, he certainly couldn't remember the feeling. Of course, at this moment he had trouble remembering his own name.

"I'm sorry about your trailer," she said, her voice sounding husky and breathless. "I didn't mean to burn it down." Ann stood still, mesmerized as Jack moved closer, drawn by that old irresistible force.

"I know. I'd be willing to overlook the fire if you provided living quarters for me," Jack offered. Now why had he said that? But the answer stood right in front of him. He sought a closer connection with Ann.

"I can't afford the price of a motel room," she whispered. Her lips moved, words emerged, surely she had thoughts, but the ideas formed on some other level because at this moment, and in this place, Ann couldn't think at all. She only felt. And the feelings seemed wonderful! And terrible! And frightening!

"You'll have to let me stay here," Jack murmured. His heart thumped a drumbeat in his chest. She was such a little thing. The top of her head barely reached his nose. She looked up at him with big blue eyes, and suddenly Jack felt about ten feet tall. He felt strong, manly, invincible. Why did she have this effect on him? He'd known a lot of women. He'd been intimate with many, but none of them ever made him feel this way. He felt like he could take on the world and win. He also felt protective of the one who stood before him now.

"Here?" Ann asked, her dazed mind not recognizing the concept. He nodded, and so did she. "Okay." The breathy sound of her voice breathed fire into his veins, raising his body heat. He moved another step closer and reached out a hand to touch her cheek. He didn't know Peanut had come back into the house until he heard the growl. He froze. So much for making friends with her dog.

The sound of her faithful watchdog's warning brought Ann out of her trance. She gave an infinitesimal shake of her head and stepped away from Jack, quietly dismissing Peanut.

Jack felt the expulsion to his bones, and he knew something important had slipped away.

"I'll pay to have your clothes replaced." A frown of concern marred Ann's brow as she spoke. "I won't be able to restore the things I destroyed with the same kind of quality, but I'll do the best I can." She became fretful.

Jack found he didn't want her plagued by anything so insignificant.

"Don't worry about my clothes." His statement seemed to calm her fears. "I don't need designer's clothes out here. If you have some more of these things, they'll do fine."

Ann turned away so Jack wouldn't see the distress his words created. She knew he thought of her as nothing but a country girl, but being told her offerings fell below his standards hurt anyway. She felt sub-human somehow at the words "out here." She retrieved the rest of her father's clothing from the trunk in her bedroom and brought them to him.

Jack sensed he'd said something wrong somewhere along the line, but he had no idea what it could have been. He wanted to bring back the easy atmosphere that had existed moments ago, but he didn't know how.

"I have work to do." She rushed into speech, fearing he'd pick up on her despair if she lingered in his company. "I expect you have a lot on your plate, too, what with the trailer clean-up." Her voice held regret for her deed, but she gave a dismissal if ever he'd heard one. And though he didn't appreciate the insult, Jack admired the poise with which she delivered it.

"Okay. I'll see you this evening, and if you'll treat me to another one of your fine dinners, I'll gladly pay for the privilege of sitting at your table."

That dumbfounded her. "You'll definitely have supper with us, but I won't accept any payment." Ann wanted that perfectly clear. "Feeding you is the least I can do."

Jack heard the sudden frost in her voice, but he didn't care. He had what he wanted. He would be sleeping in her barn and eating at her table. He would be near Ann. He'd make a friend of Haber Judd. He'd find a way to befriend Peanut, too, which would be necessary if he intended touching the dog's mistress, and Jack knew one thing for sure—he did intend to touch her.

Back on the work site, Jack began questioning his irrational decision to move in with the little hillbilly witch who'd put him under some kind of spell. In the light of day, he had difficulty believing he'd had such lustful thoughts for a woman who dressed in overalls. But even thinking the word lust in connection with Ann reminded him of how he'd felt standing close to her this morning.

He also felt guilty for allowing her to shoulder all the blame for the explosion that destroyed his trailer. After the fact, Jack remembered the small leak he discovered under the propane tank the day before the explosion. He intended to call a repairman, but he became so wrapped up in his personal probe that the leak completely slipped his mind. Jack explained all that when the police investigated the fire, but he didn't say a word to Ann.

Okay, so that made him a jerk. But he needed an excuse to stay near her. He didn't bother asking why. He couldn't, or wouldn't come up with a reason.

That was yesterday. Today, he had a very definite reason. He wanted her. His irrational behavior proved that simple. Didn't it? Not really, he admitted. Desiring intercourse with a member of the opposite sex seemed perfectly natural, but craving a woman with such forceful need existed outside his experience. All day long, he struggled with questions that had no answers.

* * * *

Ann worked the entire day as if pursued by demons. Memories of Jack and the way he made her feel this morning were the demons she attempted to escape. She tried and tried to figure out the cause for the fluttery heart and the queasy stomach, the twitchy nerve endings and the perspiration that dewed her skin.

Ann had felt some of those symptoms when she hid from her abusers, but those were the companions of fear. What she felt with Jack could not be fear. The sensations seemed too sweet and exciting to be frightening.

Was this the sexual attraction she'd read so much about in the magazines she borrowed from the doctor's office? If so, those articles terribly underrated the perfection. The feeling was the most awesome sensation she'd ever encountered. No wonder even normal people cheated and killed for one sample.

Ann wished she'd thought of a different word. The word "killed" reminded her she wasn't a normal person. Ann couldn't have a normal man-woman relationship. The lack of a man in her life never bothered her before, but now that Ann had met someone who roused her curiosity about all the fuss, it was too late. She needed to armor herself against the emotions he generated. She couldn't allow herself to hanker after the forbidden dream of love with a gentle man.

While Ann continued working and eating her heart out over Jack, he drove into town and phoned his father's office. The situation took some explaining to Mike's secretary, but she finally connected son with father. Jack asked his Dad directly if he'd sent anyone to buy the property connected with their back border.

He became disturbed when Mike told him yes; for years,

their company had been trying to convince the owner that selling to Barrister's would be advantageous. Mike told him all the first-rate reasons for wanting the extra ten acres. The acquisition made good sense from a business standpoint, if you could ignore the feelings and desires of the present owner. Jack could not, in all good conscience, do that.

Having met Ann and becoming acquainted with her, he appreciated her point of view. This was her home. If she didn't want to relocate, why should she? He felt she would be better off living somewhere else, living a different kind of life. No longer than he'd known her, Jack could see how hard she worked. He could only imagine the rest of the struggles from what Mary Jane, the store clerk, had told him.

If he could arrange Ann's life, she'd live in a nice house with a white picket fence and do nothing more all day than shop for clothes—frilly dresses and dainty shoes—and cook for him. Wait a minute! Where did that thought come from? That sounded way more serious than anything Jack had in mind.

He pulled his wits back to the business at hand and told his father about the accusations Ann leveled against their company. When he came to the part about John Harrison's courtship, Mike sounded as appalled as he had been. Just as Jack suspected, Mike never ordered, requested, or even suggested that anyone harass the property owner. He'd asked only that an offer be made every so often, adding that a bonus would be received by the person whose proposal—

business, not marriage—she accepted.

Jack remained deep in thought as he stepped out of the motel lobby and into the path of sheriff Deke Hendricks.

"Hey, Barrister. Fancy meeting you here." The big man spoke as if they hadn't just met at the helpful neighbor's house after the fire. "How's the building going."

"Fine. We're right on schedule," Jack answered, having no idea if he told the truth.

"Found a new place yet?" Deke inquired, not knowing Jack had moved into Ann's barn after the trailer burned.

Even though Jack would rather not tell him, he suddenly remembered how informative Deke had been the first time they talked about Ann. He decided to conduct some investigating of his own. "I'm staying at the Mason place until insurance adjusters give me the okay to replace the trailer," he said, tossing out the bait. He watched the sheriff's face closely, noting the smile dimmed and a frown took hold. Jack felt elated to see the big man falling into his snare.

"You staying in the house?"

He didn't say "with Ann," but Jack heard the words anyway. That, accompanied with the frown, made Jack wonder what had the man bothered. He'd figure that puzzle out when he uncovered more clues. Right now, he had a fish on the line and he started reeling him in. "I'm staying in the barn with Haber Judd," Jack paused for effect before adding, "right now."

Deke's mouth dropped open just enough for Jack to

know he'd hit a homer before the sheriff closed it and adopted a blank expression. Jack moved in for the kill before Deke recovered. "I've been thinking about the conversation we enjoyed the first time we met. Were you part of the investigating team that night at Ann's when her husband died? You never said."

"That's right, I didn't," Deke blustered. "But I led the team."

Jack didn't know if Deke would give him any more information, but he reasoned he might never have a better chance, so he persisted. "What did you see that convinced you Mason intended killing her with the shotgun instead of his fists?"

Deke narrowed his eyes. He became all watchful cop now, showing Jack the lawman side he hadn't noticed before. "The evidence at the scene left room for no other conclusion," Deke said, drawing himself up to his full six foot, six inch height.

Jack waited, unsure if Deke would let slip any more facts. His patience paid off.

"Forensics proved she lay crumpled right under him when he took the blast. His blood splattered on her and the pattern showed her exact position. The blood trail left when she dragged herself to the door showed where she had lain at his feet. Any fool could see she wouldn't have been able to go after the gun with him beating her. It stood to reason he'd been the one to fetch the firearm."

"She never said one way or the other?" Jack asked. He just

couldn't make the facts gel. He couldn't put his finger on the problem, exactly, but he knew one existed.

"The girl remained unconscious for two days. Later, when she became lucid, she didn't remember anything that happened after the third blow."

"What about Haber Judd?" he asked. "Was he there? Couldn't he tell you anything?" Jack felt frustrated to the bone. He would never make a lawman. He couldn't stand the suspense of not knowing the entire truth.

"We all hoped for that," Deke said, "but poor old Haber Judd lay out in the hen house and never heard a thing. He'd been beat up almost as bad as Ann." All of a sudden, Deke deflated. "I told her time and time again she needed to leave that tyrant, but she just shook her head and asked where she would go. That stupid father of hers willed the house to Red when the property should've been Ann's in the first place. She believed she had to stay."

"Couldn't the law do anything about this?" The injustice had Jack fuming. "Seems to me everyone in the county knew what was going on. Why didn't someone, *you*, do something?" By the time he'd finished the tirade, he was shouting. Deke looked a tad older than he did at the start of their altercation.

"You think you're the only one to ask that? I ask myself the same question every day. You weren't here. We did try. You must understand. Her dad conditioned her from birth to assume she didn't have a choice. She turned down every offer we made. You can't force a person to accept help. That's a decision only they can make."

Jack took his turn at deflating. "I'm sorry," he said sincerely. "Why anyone would let another person inflict so much pain on them is hard for me to understand. I've heard of the syndrome before, but this is the first time I've come into direct contact with spousal abuse. Thinking of a nice woman like Ann going through a lifetime of such torture hurts."

They stood for a moment, each contemplating what the other had said. Then Deke nodded, touched the brim of his hat, and walked away. Jack remained on the sidewalk in front of the motel for another few minutes before he gathered his thoughts, reeled in his temper, and headed back to work.

Finishing out the day, working in a way he never had before, Jack felt a lot of satisfaction, an accomplishment which he'd never known previously. He hated admitting Dad had been right when he said Jack never worked for anything in his life. All the good stuff came too easily, without any effort on his part.

That included relationships. Especially with women. Jack sailed through life collecting one partner after another, never thinking of their wants, their needs, or their desires aside from the obvious sexual ones. He felt pretty shallow.

Jack now faced a job that, while not exactly new, the part he played was different. He found that he liked the achievement, liked the triumphant feeling of a job well done. He thought perhaps Mike had hit a bull's eye when he said working with old Dan would straighten him out, make a man out of him.

He'd also run into a woman he didn't know how to handle. For the first time in his life, he couldn't figure out how to proceed with a female of the species. He wanted Ann, but he wanted the fulfillment of her wishes as well. He almost believed he could have a physical relationship with her, if he could convince Peanut to take a hike. Why didn't that seem like enough?

Something more bubbled in his sub-conscious. He did feel all those impressions, but another sentiment buried deep inside him struggled to make itself known. He tried to identify the emotion, but he had no comparison. Confused by the conflicting ideas, he decided he would think about the problem later. Right now, he needed to head for home. Home?

He took work home for after supper. Trying to transport the papers on the repaired Yamaha wouldn't be wise, so he drove the Hummer around to Ann's. Peanut drew his attention the minute he pulled into the drive. The dog sat on the porch by the front door. When the truck stopped, the big mongrel stood up and ambled toward it. Jack watched with trepidation as the animal neared. He sighed. Might as well take his life in his hands and face his archenemy like a man.

He opened the door and climbed out, never taking his eyes off the beast. He waited with bated breath by the truck. Peanut strolled up and sat down at his feet, tongue lolling out and tail wagging, just as if he were welcoming Jack home. Home? That thought kept popping into his mind.

Jack tentatively put his hand out and rubbed the big

shaggy head the same way he'd seen Ann do. Peanut closed his eyes in ecstasy. That went well. Maybe he and the big lummox could be friends after all. The real test would come when he tried touching Ann.

She watched the greeting between the two males from her window, and her heart swelled. Her chest felt full to bursting, and for some reason that made her feel happy. All day long she reminded herself that the baffling man planned to take her land, but the only thought that stayed in her brain was that he'd be here at suppertime. Oh, she hoped he'd be here. Standing alone, in the privacy of her kitchen, Ann could admit to herself at last that she wanted to be with him.

As he approached the house, she let her eyes drink him in. Her heart started thumping in the most alarming way. She tried to take her mind away from the fact that in seconds Jack would walk through the door. *Oh, Lordy.* That kind of thinking didn't help.

Jack opened the back door and stepped into the kitchen. There stood Ann. The minute he saw her, he knew he'd been waiting for this moment the entire day. He became swamped with a need so strong he didn't even try to fight it. He walked straight to her, leaned over, and pressed his lips against hers. Home. This was homecoming in the most elemental way. He suddenly felt safe, as if he'd entered a shelter in a storm. That idea only took a second to sink into his brain. He pulled his lips away and stared at her like she'd sprouted another head.

She turned away and started making busy work. Good

grief! One would think it was her fault he kissed her. All she did was stand there with her tongue hanging out, looking at him as if he were an ice cream sundae on the hottest day in July—ever. He probably thought she would die of deprivation if he didn't give her a peck on the mouth! She became mortified!

Regardless of her embarrassment, Ann knew deep down inside she wanted to kiss him again. She felt a blush rising in her face, blood rushing through her veins to other parts of her body. She felt heavy in some places and moist in others, and somehow she knew it had everything to do with that brief kiss.

Jack fell into a trance. Thoughts were jumping around in his head so fast he couldn't quite take hold of any specific one. He'd never felt so connected to anyone with just a little kiss. And that feeling of homecoming, what was that all about? His home was almost five hundred miles from here.

And the look on her face when he pulled back. Figure that one out. She seemed embarrassed.

Surely that couldn't be. She was a beautiful woman and a widow as well. He'd given her only a small kiss without even the slightest touch of his tongue, surely nothing new. He didn't care for that thought at all.

And why didn't Peanut have anything to say about that kiss? What kind of a watchdog was he anyway? He reminded Jack of a cop, never around when you needed him. Anyone could walk in here and kiss his mistress. Jack would have a talk with that dog.

All these thoughts flooded into his brain in an instant, but his whirling mind finally settled slowly and inexplicably on the one thing that couldn't be ignored. He had fallen in love with Ann. *He had fallen in love with Ann!*

Chapter 6

For the first time in his life, Jack felt totally helpless. He had absolutely no idea what to do. Should he tell her about his big discovery? Yeah, right! That oughta make her day. To her, he remained a stranger, one she didn't trust an inch. One she'd been working hard to weed out of her life. He needed time and space for thinking. He mumbled a couple of incoherent words and left the house.

Ann said a bad word. She'd come off looking like an idiot. He probably wondered how a woman who'd been married could be so inept at kissing. If he only knew. The man she'd called husband had never kissed her with tenderness, never held her with gentleness. But Jack would never know. Hadn't she learned anything about men from Red? She would not let herself be carried away by a bunch of hyped-up hormones, and that was that! Nevertheless, she touched a finger to her lips and savored the sensation.

When Jack reached the barn, Haber Judd had just started

in from the final chores of the day. Jack remained in a daze from the monumental discovery he'd made in the kitchen. He stood just staring into space when Haber Judd and Peanut walked in.

"Jack," Haber Judd greeted, looking at him a mite suspiciously. "Whacha doin'?" Old Haber Judd was a good judge of people, and he could tell this young man had a lot on his mind. He reckoned he should be finding out what bothered him in case his condition concerned the Mam. But Peanut also picked that time to greet Jack.

"There you are, you traitor." Jack addressed the dog that licked his hand. "Where were you when your mistress needed you?" He knelt down on one knee in front of Peanut. "We need to reach an understanding. A big guy like you should earn his keep, you know. You must stay a lot closer if you intend to keep Ann safe." Peanut licked his chin.

"Ya wanna tell me whut yer talkin' 'bout? Safe from whut?" the old man asked. Haber Judd became a mite worried now. Jack looked up at the other man as if he'd just become aware of his presence, which he had, and he rose from his kneeling position. For a while Haber Judd thought he wouldn't answer. In truth, Jack looked as if he didn't know what to say. "Whut do she need pertectin' from?" Haber Judd persisted.

"Me," Jack sighed.

Haber Judd didn't know whether to worry or feel happy. To him, what Jack said sounded a lot like love in bloom. As far as he was concerned, that created a cause for celebration. The Mam could use a little love in her life. Still, maybe he'd better not put the cart before the horse. He needed more information.

"Why'd she need pertectin' from you?" A lot rode on the answer to that question, so he listened closely in case he had to read between the lines. He watched closely, too, so he noticed when Jack heaved a great sigh.

"Don't pay any attention to me," Jack murmured. "I've really had a long day."

The words didn't tell Haber Judd anything, but the sigh gave him hope. That seed of hope came crashing down with Jack's next words.

"Hey, Haber." Haber Judd frowned because no one called him by his given name alone. "Were you around here the night Ann's husband died?"

Whatever Jack expected, it certainly wasn't the cold shoulder he received from the old man at his inquiry. Haber Judd straightened up poker stiff, turned away and walked out the door. What the... Jack ran after him.

"Hey," Jack called. He just kept walking. "Haber, what did I say?" Haber Judd stopped and turned toward Jack.

"Why ya bringin' 'at old news up fer?" he barked in that rusty nail voice. The man's black scowl should have made Jack fear for his safety, but he had a hold on something here and like a pit bull, he didn't intend to let go.

"I'm not sure, but something about the stories I'm hearing doesn't make sense," Jack mused. "And I can't stand a puzzle. I just have to solve it. Why did my question upset you so much?" Haber Judd turned his face away in order to hide his expression, but he wasn't completely successful. Jack detected a look of something. He couldn't be sure what. Fear maybe, or concern. He waited impatiently for an answer to his question.

"The Mam's had 'nough mizry over the weasel she wuz married ta. Ain't no use ta talk 'bout it no mo."

Obviously, Haber Judd didn't want to talk about the death of Red Mason, but Jack remained just as determined that he would uncover the truth. He couldn't stand the thought that Ann suffered for something she didn't do. "I can't believe Ann somehow managed to load a gun and shoot a man when, by all accounts, she couldn't even lift her arm. You tell me, Haber, where were you that night?"

Haber Judd sighed. "Ya jist ain't gonna let it go, is ya. Ya jist gotta stir thangs up. Ah mite a'swell tell ya, fore ya go get'n the story all wrong."

The old man's posture slumped and he seemed to age before Jack's eyes, making him feel some guilt for being so tenacious, but not enough to back off. "I'm all ears," Jack told Haber Judd, so the old man walked to a tree stump a few feet away and sat down.

"First thang you gotta know is Ah owe the Mam mah life. 'Bout five years back, Ah got me in a bit a trouble with dem dere white boys down in Knoxville. Ah did'n thank it wuz no big deal, but dem boys got it in they heads ta teach me a lesson. So's the four of 'um throwed me in thar car 'n hauled me up here, axuly over on yer property, 'n whooped me 'til Ah wuz out cold." He stopped talking, and a far-away look came into his eyes as he remembered that night before he continued.

"When Ah come a 'round two days later, they wuz a angel sittin' beside me. It wuz the Mam. She patched me up real good rat over thar in the ole chicken house. She said she put me thar 'cause nobody ever go's thar. Ah found out later she wuz talkin' 'bout Red. She knowed he'd kill us both if'n he learned she hept a black man." Once more that faraway look came over him, accompanied by a look of sadness. "Ah reckon he did find out. Mind ya now, he did'n need much ex-cuse ta beat on the Mam, but he wuz a plain ole niggar hater. Ah'm thinkin' he wuz plannin' on killin' 'er afore he come out fer me."

"So you were here?" Jack asked him after he'd digested some of the information. "Did you go to her aid?" Haber Judd looked at him with a puzzled expression. "Help her," Jack clarified. But the other man shook his head.

"Ah wuz still laid low out in the chicken house. Ah did'n even know whut 'e done 'til the next mornin' when the police come 'n fetched me. They toted us off ta the hospital, but Ah got out the next day." Haber Judd sighed again. "That gonna be a'nough ta keep ya happy?" he asked.

Jack sat thinking about what Haber Judd told him. His explanation did cover some of the oddities that bothered Jack, but not everything. He watched the old man walk away, and the niggling in the back of his mind just wouldn't let the issue rest. He knew there must be more to the story. He would corner Ann.

There were other things he must clear up before he could even think about giving her the third degree. But first he intended to enjoy the fine meal he could smell cooking in her kitchen. When he finished every morsel of the wonderful food her hospitality provided, he would grill her about the death of her husband.

His plans didn't work out exactly the way he anticipated. He did enjoy the food and the company. Then he helped with the clean up, and he and Haber Judd sat on the floor and listened while Ann read.

He noticed for the first time that she had trouble pronouncing a few of the words. That didn't surprise him too much since the Bible contained some of the hardest words in the English language. But a lot of the ones she labored over weren't really that difficult. He paid closer attention.

After a while he reached the conclusion that perhaps she hadn't received much in the way of a formal education. That might explain her reluctance to read in front of him. She objected last night and again this evening. Another puzzle.

Tonight he managed to stay awake until she finished, but he became so sleepy he could hardly hold his eyes open. Back in Indianapolis, he stayed up until one most nights and never thought a thing about tiredness or lack of sleep. Now at barely after nine o'clock, he was pooped.

But he really needed to talk with Ann. Who knew if they'd have a chance in the morning? So he pried his eyes open and asked if she would give him a minute. She said yes, sat back down, and settled Peanut in front of her like a shield. That action told him she meant to keep him at a distance. *For now, Honey*, he thought.

"I called my father today," he started. Ann looked at him with dread. Jack knew she thought the worst, so he quickly plunged ahead. "Dad never meant for our employees to harass you about selling your land. He didn't even know they were. He made the mistake of offering a bonus to the man who could make the purchase. That's why the guys were such eager beavers." Jack stopped talking and waited for a reaction. When one didn't come, he continued. "He's sorry for your inconvenience." No reaction.

Ann waited for the other shoe to drop. Sure, they wouldn't need persuasion to buy her land now that they had a crime hanging over her head. When he didn't continue, she knew he waited for a response from her, but she didn't know what to say. In the past, when she couldn't figure out what a man expected, doing nothing usually worked best. So that's what she did now.

"I don't want you worrying about whether someone else will come around trying to make a deal for your home," he kept plugging away. "I've taken care of everything." Still she said nothing. "Say something!" he finally said in exasperation.

"Look, Jack, I'm not a fool. I know this place is as good as yours already," she muttered. "I haven't yet figured out why you're waiting, but I know you'll make your move when you're ready, so go on."

Move? Go on? Jack had no idea what she was talking about. He'd honestly forgotten that she expected him to use that unfortunate accident with his trailer to take her property. "Are you throwing me out?" he inquired in complete ignorance. She breathed a heavy sigh.

"I'm too tired for this. I'm not asking you to leave, as you very well know. Stop pussyfooting around!" She finally cried in desperation, "We both know you have the upper hand here."

The light bulb over his head finally clicked on. "Wait a minute. You think I'm accepting your hospitality until I can have you evicted." He became so indignant, he almost yelled. "What kind of person do you think I am?" He had started yelling now. That's when Peanut registered his objections with his usual low, throaty growl. "Sorry, Peanut. But sometimes your mistress makes my blood boil!"

"I don't understand," Ann inserted into his conversation with her dog. She could see he'd become angry, or maybe just upset, but she didn't know why. "I'll admit I've been puzzled by you waiting to have me arrested, or at least use my criminal activities for convincing me to sell up and leave."

Jack's head snapped back as if she'd hit him. "I guess that tells me pretty clearly what you think of me."

He looked depressed, and Ann became even more bewildered. In her mind, he lived light years above her. It would never have occurred to her that he might be interested in her for any other reason than acquiring the only thing of value she owned, her property. "I don't understand," she repeated.

He certainly wouldn't tell her about his newly discovered love after this exhibition. Clearly he had his work cut out for him if she was ever going to return his tender feelings. He just didn't know how to go about producing that effect. He supposed he should start by dispelling her fears over ending up in jail.

"Look, let's calm down while I explain my intentions," he suggested.

Ann wanted to calm down, she embarked on trying harder, but fear of the unknown created a nerve-racking emotion. "All right," she answered and braced herself for whatever he might say.

"I haven't been completely honest with you," he began hesitantly, which probably made her even more apprehensive. "I wanted to stay here so I could become better acquainted with you. I didn't have any luck until the night I caught you messing with my dirt bike. I decided I would use the explosion incident to talk you into let me stay around. I've already told the police you weren't completely to blame."

"What!" Ann squealed. She'd been totally convinced the whole thing was her fault and hers alone. She would never have questioned it. How could he think otherwise?

"Now stay calm," he begged, knowing he treaded on thin ice here. "I haven't mentioned this before, but I discovered a small leak in the propane tank the day before you came over shooting off your shotgun, and I hadn't yet called a repairman. A good sized puddle of gas had collected under the tank and probably created a cloud of fumes. When the blast of buckshot hit the metal, sparks flew everywhere and—boom!" He decided to go for broke. "I've already cleared you with the police," he told her with a grimace.

"What!" she repeated at the top of her lungs. By now she had an effectual knowledge of exactly what he'd done and with every breath, she exhaled fire. "You mean to tell me you let me suffer the misery of thinking I'd be thrown in jail or put out of my home all this time, and the possibility didn't even exist. Of all the despicable things to do! Can you even imagine how much I've been worrying over what would become of Haber Judd and Peanut?"

She exploded out of her chair to stand right in front of him. Her chest heaved, drawing his attention to breasts which were only hinted at beneath the overalls. He raised his gaze to her face. Her eyes were shooting sparks, making them glimmer and shine like fireworks on the Fourth of July. Her skin had become flushed and rosy with her righteous indignation. Her lips parted to take in air and tempt him almost beyond control. And her dog sat between their legs emitting a low hum.

"I said stay calm," he reiterated. "I know I should have

told you earlier and I'm sorry. Please forgive me?"

He spread the charm on so thick, Ann couldn't help but eat it up. She sighed. Looking up at him didn't give her that out-of-control fear she usually felt when she stood close to a big man. In fact, her feelings were those of excitement and expectation, anticipation, wanting, desire…oh, no.

She started to step away, even though her legs wobbled so much she could hardly move, but Jack reached out and, in spite of Peanut's steady rumble, he took hold of her shoulders. Their eyes locked. They stood like that for an eternity, which lasted three seconds, before Jack spoke.

"You want to call off your dog?" he murmured. "I think he's considering taking a hunk out of my leg." He let his hands caress her shoulders just as his eyes were caressing her face.

"Peanut, sit, stay," she commanded without taking her eyes from Jack's. Her legs weren't the only things that wobbled now. Her heart floundered all over the inside of her chest. She became engulfed in curiosity. Did he intend to kiss her? If he did, would his lips on hers generate the same sensations as before? Would she like it as much?

Jack, on the other hand, had no doubts at all. He definitely intended to kiss her, she would like it, and so would he. He stepped forward and felt his clothes brush hers. He let his hands slide up her shoulders and onto her neck. The feel of her soft skin beneath his fingers seemed so incredible. He felt a rush of emotions invade his body. He couldn't wait any longer. He must taste her.

He bowed his head and pressed his lips against hers. Home. There it was again. Only this time the realization didn't startle him. He expected it, welcomed it.

Ann stood perfectly still, letting him rub her lips with his. Kissing Jack was the most wonderful thing that had ever happened to her. She couldn't imagine anything ever feeling better. Then he touched his tongue to her mouth.

Jack soared into paradise. His heart pounded out a rhythm as old as time. His blood sizzled with lust, and he became fully aroused. Even through the haze of pleasure, he realized she avoided kissing him back. He pulled away in order to see her face, to make sure she enjoyed everything he did. After all, he'd been told how her father and Red conditioned her to accept the unacceptable. He couldn't let that be the case between him and Ann.

Her eyes drifted open. Desire glowed in the depths of the windows to her soul. Jack's heart swelled with love and pride. She wanted him. He kissed her again. He rubbed his hands over her back, down around her waist, and pulled her closer.

"Open your mouth," he whispered against her lips. "Let me taste you."

Nothing had ever sounded so erotic. Powerless to resist, she opened her mouth, and felt his tongue push inside. The action should have been repulsive, which was exactly the way she felt when Red tried the same approach. But this time, the results were as different as the men. She became drenched in the most wonderful sensations—weak knees, dewy skin, excited hormones, and electrified nerve endings. She opened further, hoping for more of him, and he obliged.

He allowed his hands the freedom to caress her back, her bottom, and her sides. He let his happy fingers wander around her ribs. She moaned at the thrill of his touch. With a gasp, she opened her mouth even more, and he plunged his tongue deeper, kissing her passionately.

Ann couldn't stand, couldn't breathe, couldn't think. Totally enthralled, she wondered how she had lived twenty-three years without ever having this happen to her. Ann ran her hands over his body until a finger reached a button, and she felt a sudden urge to touch his skin. By sheer instinct, she worked one button loose, then another until she could push his shirt open, smooth her hands over his chest, delight in the feel of curly hair and warm skin.

Jack groaned with the pleasure Ann created, making her bolder. His heart thundered into triple time. Nothing in his past could compare with this. He enjoyed really making love for the first time in his life. He undid the straps of her overalls and let them fall to her waist, unbuttoned the checked work shirt she always wore and pushed his hands under the bottom of her tee shirt, caressing her skin, bringing a cry of delight.

His lips slid down her cheek to her neck and he kissed her there. Her breathing became labored, and so did his. He needed her now. He ran his hands down around her bottom and pulled her tight against him, letting her feel how affected he had become by her nearness.

Ann hadn't been thinking at all, only feeling, enjoying the wonder of these new sensations, but when Jack pulled her against him, he forced her back to reality in an instant. The impression of that hard ridge against her belly struck like a blast of ice water in her face. She began struggling.

Jack didn't immediately understand she no longer wanted his passionate advances. When the comprehension hit, he let go, even though the release hurt as if he'd severed a limb. The minute he freed her, she backed away from him as if she believed he might rape her... *Oh, my God! Had her husband done that as well?*

"Ann," he whispered huskily. "What's wrong? What did I do?" She stared at him through eyes wide with fear, and he had a sinking feeling in his stomach. "I won't hurt you. I won't do anything you don't want." He took a step toward her.

"Peanut," she cried, and the dog jumped to his feet and wedged between them before Jack could say another word. The low growl told him Peanut meant business, so he sighed and backed away.

"That wasn't necessary," he told her. "A simple 'no' would have sufficed. I don't know what you expected, but I'm not into force. I like my women willing." *Oops! Wrong thing to say.* That silver tongue had turned into dross. He could see the expression on her face changing from fear to indignation, which he actually preferred.

"I'm not one of your women," she stated emphatically. She still suffered from the aftereffects of those aforementioned

114

hyped-up hormones, and her legs were still weak, but her mind had become operational again and in control of her rebellious body. She wouldn't let her usually tepid libido rage out of control again. That she promised.

That vow proved unreliable since she didn't know what had caused the unconventional behavior in the first place. She tried to recall what she'd been doing before curiosity—yeah, that's what it was—overwhelmed her. Oh, yes. He'd been trying to convince her he wouldn't steal her land. Recognizing a clue didn't take her long.

"Am I about to receive another offer for my house now?" she asked with as much sarcasm as she could muster. She watched as surprise spread over his face, and then changed into anger. Strangely, she remained unafraid. She knew he wouldn't hurt her physically. Her emotions were the only thing she needed to worry about. *That's a bizarre suggestion*, she thought, and instantly dismissed the unwelcome notion.

"I'm going to try and forget you said that," he growled. To think she'd accuse him of ulterior motives after the mind-blowing kiss they shared hurt—bad. Didn't she feel any of the things he had felt? Evidently not.

He meant to ask her about the night her husband died, but in view of what just happened, he supposed waiting until they both calmed down would be a wiser plan. He knew he would have a hard time concentrating on anything other than her lips, red and swollen from his kisses, her young strong body causing his to vibrate, and her desire-drenched eyes. He became convinced they both needed cooling off more than anything else. He supposed he'd better leave. Jack turned without another word and walked out the door.

Peanut followed him outside and all the way to the barn. Jack thought the animal must be escorting him away from his mistress, but when he'd prepared himself and bedded down for the night, the dog came over and licked his cheek before he loped back to the house. Jack wiped his face and smiled.

He clasped his hands behind his head and thought about that wonderful embrace. He relived their fuse-blowing, mind-boggling kiss. And she had responded. She might tell herself differently, but he knew the truth. Jack could still feel the way she pressed herself against him. He could still taste her on his tongue. He could still hear her breathy sighs. She might try denying the sparks they generated, but no way under the sun would he let her get away with that.

Jack realized he faced an uphill battle. She'd experienced the worst of men and he couldn't deny being one of those. He must find a way to convince her he could never behave like the brutal specimen she married. He didn't know how he would accomplish that mission, but he remained confident he'd find a way. Jack would take one day at a time and make use of every opportunity that came his way. He might have to create a few of his own. The memory of that kiss tonight would keep him going until he had a chance to make new ones. He could hardly wait to do it again!

Her physical reticence might not be the only obstacle in the path of true love. He believed Ann's fierce pride would stand in the way of any progress he directed toward that end. He strongly suspected she would consider herself unworthy of someone who had the advantages of wealth and education. She obviously had no riches. He'd seen a few indications that Ann lacked formal schooling. He knew without a doubt that would be a huge stumbling block for her. He'd have to think on that one.

And there lingered the misunderstanding between her and his company. Proving the bond between the two of them had nothing to do with business seemed imperative. In order to accomplish that, he must somehow render her real estate off limits for his own father. Mike Barrister was a good man, a reasonable man, but when it came to the family business, he turned into a bulldog. Convincing him to drop the campaign for acquiring Ann's property would take some pretty strong motivation.

Their chances were also impeded by the mystery surrounding the death of her husband. Jack would need to question Ann about that if he wanted the tarnish removed from her sterling reputation. It seemed evident the only possibility of clearing up the matter rested with Ann.

That she trust him enough to be completely honest about that night became monumentally important to Jack. If she really couldn't recall any of the events connected with Red's death, he would move on and forget about the episode, but he needed to hear the story from her lips, or the puzzle would bug him forever. He fell asleep plotting his next conversation with Ann.

Chapter 7

The next morning didn't go according to plan. The minute he awoke, he discovered Haber Judd waiting with a request for a personal favor. He asked Jack if he would drive him into Andersonville to visit the trading post. He didn't offer an explanation, and Jack sensed the old man didn't usually ask anything of anyone, so he told him he would be glad to give him a lift. Jack informed Haber Judd he also needed a few things, but they must stop by the construction site so he could check in and let Dan know where he would be.

Breakfast began as a quiet affair. Jack had the surprising thought that Ann might be embarrassed about last night. He found the idea charming and refreshing after his associations with more sophisticated women who thought nothing of casual encounters. He felt proud of her.

At the same time, her old-fashioned standards made him feel ashamed of his past lifestyle. He knew he'd lived more like the rest of the world than she had, but that didn't make his standards the right ones. The concept was a new idea for him, and one that made a lot of sense in a day and age where sexual promiscuity sometimes proved dangerous, even deadly.

After he stuffed himself with another lip-smacking breakfast, he and Haber Judd made their excuses and left for their adventure in town. On the way, Jack tried starting up a conversation, but met with monosyllabic answers until he asked Haber Judd point blank why he requested a ride when Jack knew he could drive. Haber Judd smiled. Jack had never seen that particular expression on his face.

"The Mam's birthday's ta-mara. Ah been savin' all year ta buy 'er a book, 'n Ah said Ah'd fetch it taday," the old man stated, beaming ear to ear.

Jack found the transformation of the dour face to a boyish countenance intriguing. "Ann's birthday! I'll have to buy her something." Jack said, smiling back. "What do you think she'd like?" He grew surprised when Haber Judd's happy smile dimmed a bit.

"Doubt she'll take a gift from ya," he murmured in that rusty nail voice, "but if'n she did, Ah reckon she'd lack most anythang, so long as it wud'n too cosly. She's got a powerful lotta pride."

Jack glanced at him, then back to the road. Yes, he knew about that pride and still stewed over finding a way around it. "Will you help me pick something out?" When silence met his request, he sneaked another look in Haber Judd's direction.

The man stared wide eyed at him as if he'd just suggested they sprout wings and fly the rest of the way to Andersonville. "What?" Jack cried. He was amazed when the black man's skin darkened even more.

"Ah reckon ya don't know whut yer askin'," he replied. "Ah 'spect thangs is different up north whur ya'll come from, but round heah a black man's gotta be mahdy careful 'bout whur 'e duz 'is bizness."

"Are you telling me the stores around here won't sell to black people?" Jack double-checked in order to make sure he understood the message, appalled at the idea. Haber Judd was right. His circle of friends included several races, and he'd never known any one of them deprived of the privilege of spending their money anywhere they wished. Of course, they all had a lot of money. What if they didn't? Would that limit the places they'd be allowed to shop? *Hmm...*

"You take me wherever you're most comfortable," Jack finally answered, and judging by the look of wonder on Haber Judd's face, he just might have made a friend.

He parked the truck in the designated spot and followed Haber Judd into the ally. At the back entrance of the trading post, Haber Judd stopped and knocked on the door. Mary Jane answered shortly. She acted friendly enough when she saw Haber Judd and very surprised when she spied Jack behind him.

She asked if they would wait a minute and left them standing in the dingy ally. When she returned, she had a small bag which she handed to Haber Judd.

"I hope she likes the book," she told him with a smile.

Jack understood that Mary Jane knew the present was intended for Ann. He became further surprised when Haber Judd respectfully asked, "Ya got som'um fittin' fer Jack ta give ta the Mam?"

She looked at Jack and smiled the same way she'd done for Haber Judd. "I'll be right back," she assured them and disappeared into the store. She returned minutes later carrying a catalogue which she handed out and instructed them to knock again when they were ready. Jack first became flabbergasted. Then outraged.

"She can't treat you like this," he bellowed. "Come on, we're going inside!" He'd turned and started for the front of the store when Haber Judd grabbed hold of his arm.

"Naw sir," he said insistently "Don't make no trouble. Ya jist don't git it. We gotta stay heah after ya'll go home. If Ah raise a ruckus, the stink rubs off on the Mam. Ah won't have it." He moved himself in front of Jack and stood his ground.

"But that's not fair," Jack sputtered, "You have as much right to go into that store and buy what you want as anyone else." His anger reached the boiling point. His blood pressure had surely climbed over three hundred. He was about one degree away from exploding.

As the angry red haze began to clear, he saw a tear leak from Haber Judd's eye, and he realized the man had lived with this kind of injustice all his life. The thought sobered Jack. He reached out and placed his hand on his new friend's shoulder.

"All right, we'll do things your way," he said, and they headed back down the alley to wait for Mary Jane.

Haber Judd took a minute to pull himself together, and then he turned to Jack. "Thank ya," the old man said with gratitude glowing in his eyes. "Ain't no other white folk ever stood up fer me that way, 'ceptin' the Mam. Ah jist thought she wuz special. Ah reckon they's more of ya than Ah knowed."

Jack felt humbled. He'd never in his life considered ordinary things—like shopping where you want—an important event. Now he'd never be able to look at such an everyday occurrence in the same light. He became forever changed.

They poured over the catalogue twice and finally settled on a tablet of paper with a pretty design on the cover. Jack argued it seemed a poor present, but Haber Judd kept insisting Ann would never accept the gifts he wanted to buy for her. So they finally knocked on the door and made the purchase. Jack did have the small offering gift-wrapped and Haber Judd agreed wholeheartedly. He said Ann would be overjoyed at the bright paper and shiny ribbon because she'd never had a store wrapped present before. Jack found that incredible.

He thought he learned a great lesson of life during that hour they spent in the ally, but as Jack and Haber Judd stepped out into the street, he found he'd only begun to see the problems a black person might face in a small southern town.

They were knee deep in discussion about the best way to offer Ann her gifts the next day when a raucous laugh drew their attention. Only a few yards away stood three rough looking young men who were eyeing them with distaste. They were armed. Jack didn't like the look of this. Neither did Haber Judd.

"Well, well, look what we got here," one of the ruffians crowed. "Looks like a nigger lover and his 'boy.'"

As he eyed three malicious smiles, a feeling of dread washed over Jack. He maintained a fit body, and Haber Judd preserved his muscles, too, but a rifle and two shotguns were bad news no matter what shape you were in.

They started toward the Hummer without uttering a word; each knowing retreat had become the better part of valor. They'd only traveled a few feet when one of the tormentors placed himself in front of them.

"Don't ya recognize a insult when ya hear one," the lout called noisily.

Jack looked him right in the eye, ignoring the other two men he knew were behind them. "I recognize an uneducated ignoramus when I see one," he said with bravado he didn't actually feel at the moment. "And I'm looking at one right now." He tossed that in for good measure. The hooligan's eyes narrowed and his mouth worked for a second before he could control his vocal cords.

"I think we got us one of them smart-alecky city slickers here, that's what I think." He smirked. "Whadda' you guys think?"

There came murmurs of agreement from behind, and

Jack figured he and Haber Judd were dead meat. If everyone else here thought like these wise guys, they couldn't expect any help from the townspeople. Ann had remained out at her place working. Dan had probably run into Norris or stayed out at the site. It looked as if they were on their own.

The one in front took a step toward them, and Jack mentally prepared to receive a major hurt.

But the door of the trading post burst open, and Mary Jane pointed a double barreled shotgun in their direction.

The spunky lady shouted, "I might not be able to kill you with this buckshot from all the way over here, but you can bet your sweet bippie you're gonna bleed a lot."

Jack's mouth fell open in shock. Haber Judd's did, too. They didn't have a chance to move or speak before another voice joined hers.

"What she don't make bleed, I will," said the six foot six, big-as-a-barn sheriff. "I think you 'boys' are coming along with me. The county will be charging you with public intoxication, public intimidation with a fire arm, terrorism, smelling bad, and anything else I can think of. Haber Judd can add any personal charges he wants." Deke Hendricks gave Haber Judd a questioning look, but the black man shook his head.

Jack stood, amazed. He'd been so concentrated on the punk in front of him that he remained totally unaware of anything else. Now he looked around and saw at least four people with weapons in hand, obviously meant as protection for him and Haber Judd.

"I don't understand," he muttered as Deke herded the ruffians toward his vehicle, and Mary Jane came within hearing distance. "You're willing to protect him, but you won't let him shop in your store."

She looked extremely offended. "You got the wrong end of the stick, Son," she huffed. "It's Haber Judd that won't come in the store. He knows there's still a few of these rednecks around, and they're just looking for a reason to start on anyone they consider weaker. He's determined not to give them any grounds for doing what they're already itching to do. I humor him." She paused and smiled brightly at them. "Y'all have a real good day now. Hear?" With that, she hiked the gun over her shoulder, and walked back into her store. Jack turned to Haber Judd.

"I guess there are more white people willing to go to bat for you than me and Ann," he stated, eyeing the man beside him. He seemed as surprised by the display of support as Jack. "How have you lived here so long and not known how much these good people like you?"

Haber Judd stood there on the sidewalk, fascinated by what had happened. He slowly realized the Mam probably didn't know any more about the friendliness of these people than he did. A big grin spread over his face. This was a major revelation. He couldn't wait to tell her.

Jack left his companion storing the packages in the truck and followed Deke to the squad car where he stood talking into the radio phone. He'd called for help in transporting the rabble-rousers to the county jail.

"If a person wanted to find out the details of an old investigation on a closed case, how would he go about it?" Jack asked the lawman his question as soon as he hung up.

Deke's momma didn't raise no dummies. He narrowed his eyes and stared at Jack for a full minute before he answered. "You're talking about Red Mason, aren't you? Why would a person go poking around in old news like that?"

Haber Judd said almost those exact words. Jack shrugged his shoulders. "Curiosity?" He could tell Deke didn't buy that load of bull, but he didn't really care. He just wanted the truth.

"Have you talked to Ann about this?" Deke queried.

"Not yet," Jack told him as he watched every flicker of expression on the other man's face. He saw something there, he just knew it! But he couldn't justify, even to himself, why he believed that.

"Talk with Ann," the big man told him. "If she can't tell you what you want to know, you could always go over to the county Sheriff's office and ask for the official report. Someone there will help you."

Jack understood that Deke meant the help wouldn't come from the sheriff himself. That just made the puzzle more fascinating.

Jack decided this would be as good a time as any for telling his Dad to leave Ann alone, so he asked Haber Judd if he could wait another minute and stepped inside to use the payphone. Forty-five minutes later he walked from the store with a grim expression on his face. Swaying his father to his side took every bit of his charm and finesse, and he'd been forced to admit he harbored strong feelings for the woman. But he finally convinced Mike to halt any schemes designed for persuading Ann to sell her land. At least temporarily.

Mike left him with the impression that a lot depended on his success, or lack of it, with romancing Ann. His parents had been after him to settle down for a long time. Maybe they'd caught a whiff of victory and were so overjoyed with the idea they weren't even going to request a meeting with the bride, as long as she became his.

He couldn't blame Mom and Dad. He felt the same way. He hoped when he told Ann about his talk with Mike, she'd be a lot more susceptible to his persuasion. Ann becoming his wife was all he could think about on the way home.

Jack dropped Haber Judd at Ann's and headed over to the site. In a fairly short time, he'd become accustomed to falling into bed early, rising early and starting the job early. He grew more and more proud of his new attitude and work ethics. He no longer minded admitting his Dad had been right. This kind of discipline was just what he had needed all along. This, and Ann.

That day he spent a good deal of time mentally preparing himself for the coming discussion about Red's death. He intended suggesting they go to the county sheriff's office and request a look at their reports. He remained adamant about clearing her name. Her gratefulness would surely smooth the way for him to woo her. And woo her he would, because he wanted love, not gratitude.

That evening he enjoyed listening as Haber Judd told Ann the story of their morning-in-town experience. The older man still felt overjoyed at the fact that so many of the town's people were willing to take up weapons in his defense. Even though Jack felt sure he'd already told Ann at least once, clearly he delighted in telling the story again. Jack had never heard him talk so much.

When he'd eaten his fill of steak and potatoes and started working on a large piece of apple pie, Jack decided the time had come to bring up the forbidden subject.

"I talked to Deke Hendricks today after the showdown." He began with all the confidence in the world that his plan would be well-received. "He told me you don't remember what happened the night Red died." He stopped speaking and looked at his two listeners. Haber Judd had suddenly found something on his plate that required his complete concentration, and Ann became intent on chewing that piece of pie into mush. Wide-eyed, she nodded her head. Curious.

"I thought we might go over to the sheriff's office and look into the official records," he continued, positive any suggestion that helped put her in the clear would be met with jubilation. "We could go tomorrow if you're free. The reports might contain data that wouldn't mean anything to the men who investigated, but you would find familiar. If nothing else,

we might uncover information that would jar your memory."
He searched the faces of his dinner companions. Haber Judd
still had his head bowed over his plate. Ann looked as if she
tried to swallow a watermelon. Neither answered right away.
Curiouser.

"I'm sorry, I can't go anywhere tomorrow," Ann finally
croaked, almost choking on that ground up bite of pie. "We start
planting in the morning." Jack couldn't think of a thing to say.

He looked at Haber Judd whose nose almost touched his
plate by now. What was going on?

"I don't understand. Don't you want to know what happened? Wouldn't you like to clear the whole mess up once
and for all?"

"Has the likelihood there's nothing to clear up ever occurred to you?" Ann muttered, raising her voice enough to let
Jack know she had become upset.

The reaction he'd hoped for hadn't taken place. She as
good as admitted she killed the man. That scenario proved unacceptable. He could sanction that theory if the story sounded
true. After all, the scum deserved a horrible end. But Jack
couldn't see any possible way that Ann could have done the
deed. No, she couldn't have shot Red.

"Look, I only want to help," Jack murmured, trying to
smooth the feathers he'd ruffled. "It's no big deal. We'll just
go and have a look. We won't even tell anyone why we're
there." He waited for a positive response.

"If you really want to help, stay out of my business." Ann

looked more upset by the second. "Just leave me alone," she ordered. "I've lived with distrust and suspicion for five years. It won't kill me to go on living with it." She rose from the table and started clearing up.

Jack sat quietly on his chair, not knowing what to say. He never dreamed she would turn him down. He moved through the nightly ritual of washing and putting away the old dishes, and listening while Ann read, but his mind was distracted from the soothing words. Thoughts of those police records and proving Ann's innocence took the prominent place in his head. He sat on the floor beside Haber Judd, mentally making plans to head for the Anderson County Sheriff's office as soon as he could.

When Ann finished reading, and the men were on their way to the barn, Jack decided he would tackle Haber Judd about why the dinner conversation fizzled. Both their attitudes baffled Jack, and he couldn't stand an unsolved puzzle.

"Why do you think Ann's so dead set on leaving all this doubt about Red's death as it is? Wouldn't you think she'd want the matter cleared up?" Surprise filtered through Jack when the old man said nothing. "You do think she's innocent, don't you?"

That old Tennessee moon didn't give enough light for distinguishing Haber Judd's facial features, so Jack couldn't read his expression, but his silence spoke volumes. Jack experienced a sinking sensation in the pit of his stomach. His heart began racing.

"You don't think she killed him!" he squeaked. Haber

Judd kept walking. "Tell me," Jack shouted, rounding in front of the older man. Haber Judd let out a long sigh.

"The Mam ask ya ta leave it be," he said as he scooted around Jack and continued on toward the barn. "'At's good 'nough fer me."

Jack's temper climbed.

"The two of you give no one a choice but to think she's guilty. No wonder the whole county believes she killed Red!" Jack yelled at Haber Judd's retreating back. "Is that what you want? Do you want her to live the rest of her life branded a murderess?"

As he stopped and watched Haber Judd disappear into the barn, Jack became swamped with frustration. He'd never been so stymied in his life. What was wrong with these people? Why didn't they want to help him find the truth? *Unless they already know the truth*, he thought, *and don't want anyone else knowing*.

No, he wouldn't, couldn't accept that. She was incapable of murder. But what else could Red's death have been? He decided he couldn't count on either of them helping in his investigation. He would solve the puzzle on his own.

Jack remained completely unaware of the heartaches he'd unleashed with his persistence in dragging out a long dead incident. He ignored everyone's reluctance to pursue the idea that Ann might not be guilty, running rough-shod over their unwillingness to help and pretty much insisting on having his way.

In town today, Deke tried to put him off without offering assistance. If Jack hadn't asked point blank where he might obtain information, the lawman would've left him in the dark even though Jack believed Deke cared about Ann's well being.

And he expected Haber Judd would jump at the chance of helping "the Mam" in any way he could. Instead, he'd clammed up and refused to talk about her dilemma at all. What on earth could make a loyal friend like Haber Judd walk away from seeking to find any truth that would help Ann?

Ann's attitude proved even stranger. One could almost believe she wanted things just the way they were.

Jack couldn't know that in the barn Haber Judd's heart broke all over again, as it had so many times before. He hated his inability to assist the woman who'd helped him so much. He'd come to Ann beaten, bruised, skin and bone, a homeless vagrant without a thing to recommend him. She'd found him, nursed him, fed him, and protected him. She'd saved his sanity and his life. How could he not do everything in his power to help her?

In the house, Ann prepared for bed and worried. She remembered the expression on Jack's face, and she grew certain he hadn't been deterred from his course of action. She must find a means of keeping him away from that particular area of her life. She would have a talk with sheriff Deke, if she thought it would do any good, but that would probably just start him up again. He'd never been satisfied with the lack of closure after Red's death, but he'd finally accepted the absence of an explanation. He might even reopen the case if Jack started digging around. That was all she needed.

Oh, but Jack had awakened such wonderful dreams with his talk of clearing her name, and his belief in her innocence, and his chocolate brown eyes shining with excitement for the chase after truth...

That's all his ideas would ever be, a dream, because she could never tell a single soul what really happened that night. They would just have to continue with their speculation. That secret she would take to her grave.

Her secret remained the strongest reason she couldn't let Jack come too close. He was the kind of man who would never give up once his curiosity had been aroused. The farther away from him she stayed the better for all concerned. He would quickly forget his interest in her once he returned to Indiana. Out of sight, out of mind. She just hoped absence didn't make her heart grow fonder. She didn't know if she could stand the pain.

Ann tried settling into sleep, but something had her worried. Why did she care what Jack thought of her? And when did she start caring? He meant nothing to her except a problem. True, he turned out to be a lot nicer than she'd expected, and he looked handsome, but he was still a man. And she didn't trust men. A little voice reminded her that her two best friends were males. They might be different species, but they were both males.

One of those males padded his way into the room and over to the bed. Peanut laid his big black head on the pillow beside her face and licked her nose. Ann laughed. She imagined that lick told her everything would turn out fine. She hoped the dog was right.

But right or not, her fate had been decided the night Red died. While she claimed no happiness over his death, she certainly wouldn't wish him back. He'd made her life a living torment. Even beyond the physical pain, he controlled every aspect of her existence. He dictated when she slept, what and when she ate, what she wore, and when she worked. Sometimes she worked even when she was sick as a dog because if she stopped, she received a beating. Life became a little easier when she obeyed.

She promised herself on awakening in the hospital no one would ever have that kind of control over her again. She would live alone, be her own boss, and control her own destiny as much as life and the world would allow.

Ann fell asleep with that refrain running through her mind, but in her dreams Jack came singing a song of love and joy such as she had never known. The melody became a siren's song that drew her to him. She floated on currents of sweetness and light until, right before she reached his outstretched hand, an evil wind blew her toward a black hole. She struggled to reach Jack, but she drifted further away until he became a dot and the darkness and malevolence of the hole surrounded her. She cried out, awaking from the nightmare. Shaking with emotions of fear and defeat, she lay staring at the ceiling until time to start her day.

Chapter 8

Jack noticed the tension in the kitchen the next morning. Haber Judd remained just as uncommunicative as he had been in the barn prior to coming inside. Ann stayed so busy she didn't have a spare minute for sitting down and eating. Of course, she kept doing the same things over and over. Jack knew she worked to avoid talking with him.

He tried making conversation and acting naturally, but he soon grew as tense as the other two. Peanut seemed the only one unaffected by yesterday's events. He greeted everyone joyously and equally. On the other hand, maybe the big dog had more intellect than the humans and knew forgetting about their differences would be best. Or maybe he was just a better actor.

Jack and Haber Judd had entered the house intent on celebrating Ann's twenty-fourth birthday, and they wanted to start her special day off right. They left their gifts outside the door on the way in just as they'd planned yesterday coming home from Andersonville. Even though the affair fell short of the jubilant occasion he'd anticipated, Jack stayed determined to create a festive air for her enjoyment. He and Haber Judd insisted Ann take a seat at the table as soon as they cleared away breakfast, and they sang Happy Birthday to her. She looked thunderstruck at the sound of Jack's baritone and Haber Judd's rusty nails singing just for her.

While she sat there stunned beyond words, the two men brought in their gifts and presented them to the birthday girl. Tears began flowing as she unwrapped the crudely put-together package from Haber Judd, who'd refused Jack's offer to have it gift wrapped. When she saw the book, she cried out her joy and surprised both men by jumping up, throwing her arms around Haber Judd's neck, and giving him an excited hug.

Then she turned her eyes upon the beautifully wrapped contribution from Jack. He took pleasure in the awed expression on her face as she beheld the first elegantly wrapped gift she had ever received. As he watched, she drew a sharp breath and her eyes flew to his. He grew entranced by her apparent wonder. With nothing but bright paper and shiny ribbon, he'd produced that look of joy and rapture. He felt humbled.

Ann finally tore her gaze from Jack and took the gift he offered. She carefully and painstakingly untied the ribbon and pulled the plastic tape away from the paper without a single tear. When she opened the wrap and discovered the lovely tablet inside, she squealed with happiness and hugged her prize to her breasts. She thanked him profusely in lieu of the embrace he'd hoped to receive. Jack grew jealous of that tablet's position.

He also felt humbled by a display that showed him how easy and blessed his life had been. He couldn't imagine any one of his acquaintances getting excited by such a gift, let alone the wrappings. Even his niece and nephews were past the stage where they became thrilled by such simplicity.

With a big, bright smile and the happiest look he'd ever seen on her face, Ann thanked them again and again for the gifts and the kind thoughtfulness. But inevitably, the tension returned, bringing the celebration to an end.

Jack left as soon as he finished helping clear the birthday clutter away. Jack had learned well. He checked in at the site, talked with old Dan, explained that he needed to run an errand, and asked if he could have the morning for personal time. With Dan's blessings, he took off for Norris to check in at the county sheriff's office.

Ann hadn't lied when she said the planting must be done, so she began burying seeds while Haber Judd checked his trap to see if he'd caught a rabbit for that evening's supper. If he found the trap empty, he would go fishing before he began helping in the garden. Experience taught him the fish would bite better early in the morning or too late in the evening for their meal.

Jack arrived at his destination where officers of the law greeted him with reserved handshakes. The men had obviously been instructed to co-operate and in no time at all he sat at a worn pine table beneath a barred window. A thick folder lay in front of him.

Opening the file felt like a betrayal, knowing Ann had asked him not to meddle. Nevertheless, he felt his interference served a greater purpose, so he forced his fingers to turn the outer page and begin the search.

Reading the documents proved a slow undertaking. Some of the dialogue became technical in nature and difficult for a layman to understand. But Jack considered himself a smart guy with a college education. After a fraught half hour, the gobbledygook started arranging itself into something resembling the English language, and he began absorbing at least a portion of what he read.

The details were grisly. He'd never read an actual account of a crime before. The only experience he possessed in that direction came from television, movies, and books. In other words, fiction. This proved quite different.

As he rooted out understandable words from the police jargon, one thing became perfectly clear. The crime scene had been a bloodbath. And there were pictures. Jack came dangerously close to losing his breakfast.

Everything he'd been told, the pictures portrayed. Shotgun shells lay on the floor beside the overturned box they'd come in. The body of a man lay in a pool of blood, his face pretty much destroyed by a shotgun blast. In spite of unidentifiable features, all reports concluded the body was that of Red

Mason. There were pictures of blood spatter patterns on the floors and walls all around him. Jack saw the trail of smeared blood where Ann had dragged herself to the door. Using only the photos, determination of where her blood ended and Red's began proved impossible.

He flipped the page and the next photograph came in sight. It portrayed Ann, but an Ann he couldn't recognize. Even though the pictures were in black and white, her face looked bloody, swollen, and bruised. Not one space bigger than a square inch remained unblemished. The horrible sight became embedded in Jack's brain.

On top of that, her clothes were ripped and torn, barely hanging on her skinny body, and exposing more carnage. Through the rips in the cloth he could see rips in her flesh. The angles of her limbs revealed broken bones. She had the look of death.

That sight drove everything else from Jack's mind. Tears dripped down his cheeks, and his heart broke in two. If the pictures had not showed the man already dead, Jack would be up and looking for him right now. No wonder everyone said Red deserved his gruesome demise.

Jack rose from the table and stumbled out of the room. He walked unsteadily past concerned officers who tried to inquire after his well being. He stepped out of the building in a stupor and gazed around unseeing. He felt sick to his stomach, so he ducked into an ally and threw up. He didn't feel any better, only less nauseous.

He wished he'd never gone in there, never seen those pictures. He wished he could wipe their memory out of his mind. Everyone tried to tell him to leave the situation alone, but did he listen? No. He had been so stubborn and cocksure of himself. Now the fear grew that he would never be free of the images portrayed in those photos.

Jack climbed in the truck and sat motionless until he became stable enough to drive. He headed toward the lake, but not the building site. Instead, he visited the docking area that would become part of the resort someday and sat watching the water, grateful for its calming effect. Finally he felt recovered enough to go back to work.

He made it through the rest of the day by sheer will. He breathed a sigh of relief when the time came to quit. Now he could go off by himself and let his emotions loose. He jumped on his dirt bike and started roaming the hills. Racing up and down and around the Tennessee mountains at lightning speed proved therapeutic. Sun on his face and wind in his hair worked wonders at taking his mind off the crime evidence he had viewed this morning.

Had he looked at those pictures only this morning? It seemed a lifetime ago. All the silly things he'd done in his twenty-nine years mocked him. Now, Jack recalled the days when he thought of getting high on alcohol as a dangerous pastime. He'd never known danger. He realized that now, and he celebrated the fact. He'd been deprived of nothing and protected from much. Thank God!

But Ann had been protected from nothing. The kind of life she'd been forced into remained inconceivable for Jack.

Coming full circle, he stopped the dirt bike at the back of his property, and walked into the woods toward Ann's house. Contemplation of her and the life she had tolerated humbled him once again. The minute he returned home, he would fall on his knees and thank his mom and dad for being his parents.

He'd walked almost to her property boundary when he sensed someone else's presence. After viewing those crime scene pictures, he had become easily spooked and very defensive. He spun around, ready to protect himself, but only Haber Judd appeared.

Old Haber Judd eyed the younger man critically and knew at once something bad had happened. He motioned for Jack to follow and led the way to a fallen tree where they sat down.

"Ya went taday, did'n ya?" he questioned. Jack nodded, but said nothing. "Ya seen them pitchers? Ya seen how she looked?" Again Jack nodded. So did Haber Judd. For a while neither spoke, both lost in their own deep thoughts. Finally, without apparent reason, Haber Judd began speaking of his life before Ann.

"Ah had me a family once," he started and Jack became riveted by the look on his face. "Mah woman took mah young'ens 'n left me when the drinkin' got ta be too bad. Ever time Ah made a dollar, Ah spent sebumdy cents fer licker. Finely, she jist could'n take no more 'n she up 'n left.

"Ah did'n blame 'er none, but Ah miss 'er turrible. Ah dranked more'n ever after she went 'til Ah ended up sleepin' in the street. Ah did'n have no home, no clothes, no food, no nothin'. But Ah did'n much care, so long as Ah could git a drink or beg a dollar. Ah wuz a skinny, dirty shell of a man. 'At's when dem white boys went 'n made a ig-zample of me, said people needed ta know whut happen ta trash left layin' in the street. So's they brung me up here 'n beat me half dead. Left me layin' in the road jist over by yer place." He indicated the direction with a wave of his hand. The faraway look in his eye informed Jack he had become caught up in reliving the incident.

"Ann saved you that day, didn't she?" Jack asked, even though he already knew the answer.

"Night," Haber Judd corrected. "It wuz night 'n the Mam tells me the moon wuz a'shinein' ta beat sixty. She said it sure hept 'er git'n me back ta her place with that old moon a shinein' so bright." He smiled. "Could'n prove it by me. Ah wuz stuck in the back seat with two of dem boys sit'n on me. Ah could'n see a thang. 'Sides, Ah wuz so sceert Ah could'n see mah hand in front a mah face." He actually laughed. Jack stared, intrigued.

"After that, how much time passed before Red died?" Jack dared to question. Haber Judd looked as if he'd enjoy teaching Jack a lesson like "dem boys" taught him.

"Reckon it wuz about two days bafore he knowed she had me stashed in the chicken house," he muttered, not too happy with this line of questioning.

Jack thought of those photos again.

"She must have made a lot of noise. You know, screamed and cried, wouldn't you think?" Even saying those words made him hurt again. Jack waited for an answer, but he didn't really expect Haber Judd to give one.

"Yeah, probly did," the old man said. He might be an uneducated man, but he was smart. He knew exactly where this conversation headed, yet he didn't do a thing to divert it.

"Did you hear her?" Jack asked quietly. He felt compelled to ask the question even though he doubted he wanted the answer.

"Yeah," Haber Judd whispered. "Ah reckon Ah did." The old gentleman pulled himself up mentally. "Must'a been toward the end though, cuz the sound of the shotgun goin' off come purdy quick after that. 'Bout drove me crazy waitin' for somebody ta come 'n tell me whut wuz hap'nen. Maybe it wuz a blessin' Ah wuz in such a bad shape. He'd a done me in good if'n Ah'd a been able ta git up ta the house."

Jack considered all that information. In spite of everything he'd been told and everything he'd seen, something still didn't ring true.

"Come on," Haber Judd said. "Time ta git ta supper." They rose and started walking through the woods in silence. Jack continued wrestling with a lot of facts that didn't gel. His Daddy always told him if two and two didn't make four the answer was probably five. He believed this looked like a five.

Jack thought on all these things as they washed up and headed in the house. The minute he walked in the door and saw her, he became saturated in such stringent emotions he couldn't speak. He continued staring at her until she stared back. In his mind's eye, Jack saw Ann as she had been that night, bruised, broken, and bleeding. The horror rose up inside, overwhelming him. He excused himself and hurried out the back door in case he threw up again.

Jack waited around the corner until Haber Judd and Peanut came out of the house. As they started toward the barn, he approached the door and knocked. She opened it immediately.

"May I come in," he asked in a gravelly voice. "We need to talk." She didn't speak, but nodded her head and opened the door wider so he could step inside. Jack couldn't take his eyes off her face. It looked so different from the one in the pictures. He searched for evidence of the misery she'd endured, and even in the dim light, he could detect tiny scars. He fought off tears.

"I saved you some food." She spoke hesitantly, not knowing his reason for missing supper or why he stared at her so intently. He swiftly covered the few feet that separated them, pulled her into his arms, and buried his face in her hair. He still struggled to contain the tears that threatened.

This performance from Jack took Ann completely off guard. She stiffened her body at first, until she became aware of the tremors coursing through him and the noise he made that sounded suspiciously like a sob. Her concern for him let her relax. She slid her arms around his waist and held him.

"I love you," she heard him say. Shock paralyzed her. In her entire life, no one had spoken those words in connection with her. Ann's brain flew into overload. She couldn't think rationally. Her nerves were sending jumbled signals. She pushed against his chest until he moved back, but she looked at him without really seeing.

"I'll fetch your food," she mumbled, but didn't make a move toward the stove.

Jack tried to read the expressions that flashed across her face. Surprise became evident, and wariness, and a bit of fear, but he also saw something that gave him encouragement. He detected a hint of fascination, interest—and possibly hope?

"Ann," he whispered, and put his hands out toward her, but she backed away one step. He took two steps forward. They heard the flap of the doggie door and Peanut came in wagging his tail and begging for attention. He didn't receive any. They were totally concentrated on each other. So, Peanut lay on the floor and observed.

"What do you want?" Ann's muddled brain finally allowed her to ask. "I can't give you anything. I have nothing to give." She stopped and drew a breath because her lungs had contracted, and she couldn't inhale enough oxygen. "Please," she pleaded, but she had no idea what she asked for.

"I won't hurt you," he murmured. "I just want to hold you. Let me." Her back rested against the old cabinet and she couldn't move any farther away. He took one more step and their clothing touched.

Suddenly the room seemed stifling. Ann gasped for breath, thinking she might die from lack of air, but somehow she didn't.

Jack leaned forward and pressed his lips against hers. With just that touch, muscles lost their strength. She felt weak as water. Her legs could hardly hold her up. She clutched his shirt to keep from folding. Her lids grew heavy, so she closed her eyes.

He felt her sliding away and caught her up against him. Holding her close, he delighted in the feeling of completeness. Nothing had ever felt like this. Nothing he'd ever done excited him as much as standing in this country kitchen holding this particular woman, barely touching, barely kissing. He wondered what would happen when they actually made love. He just might die of happiness.

Ann suspected she was already dying—of pleasure. This felt even more intense than the last time. How could that be possible? She'd thought nothing could ever feel better than their first kiss. What else had she been missing out on all these years? Ideas and impressions whirled at tornado speed through her sub-conscious, but her conscious mind stayed totally involved in the sublime moment.

Jack pulled his mouth from hers and once again buried his face in her hair. They stood that way for several minutes, just holding each other lightly, breathing deeply and letting their emotions settle into something resembling calmness. Finally Jack spoke.

"Did you hear what I said?" he whispered into her hair. "I love you." He turned his head until his mouth rested against her ear. "I love you." He hoped for a similar confession from her, but instead she shook her head.

"No, you don't. You can't."

She sobbed, and he realized she was crying. He didn't understand, but he had a feeling he'd better be finding out. At that moment, he heard Peanut's steady, throaty growl, bless his little heart. He disentangled himself from his loved one just enough to view her troubled, tear drenched face. Her anxiety made him love her even more.

"I'm a grown man," Jack murmured as he used his thumbs to wipe moisture from her cheeks. "I know what I feel. I can tell you without a doubt that I've never felt like this before." He watched as she continued shaking her head. "What makes you think I don't love you?"

Ann turned away, using the sleeve of her shirt to finish mopping her face. She couldn't go very far with the cabinet top pressed against her tummy and Jack's very distracting touch all along her back.

"You just feel sorry for me," she cried softly. "I guess you've been to the police station. I hear they have pictures of the way I looked that night. I've heard they're pretty graphic, even gruesome. I didn't want you to see that. Why couldn't you leave the mess alone?" She scooted around him and crossed the room, putting the table and Peanut between them. But Peanut licked Jack's hand and wagged his tail. The table constituted a bigger threat.

"You're right. I did go to the sheriff's office today. And I did see the pictures. I can't deny the sorrow I feel knowing you had to go through that," Jack told her honestly. "Yet you survived and came out stronger and better. But that's not why I said I love you. I've been fascinated by you from the beginning. I don't think I ever told you, but the first time I saw you, you were out behind the house digging in the dirt with a garden rake. I didn't know a woman could do that. I admit I couldn't figure out why I found you so interesting at the time. I thought you captivated me because you were different from all the other women I'd known. Now I realize I became attracted to you way back then. I just didn't recognize the magnetism. I believe you're innocent of any wrong doing. Together we can prove it." He hoped for a positive reaction to his suggestion, but as he watched, her face closed up.

His words were a death toll for the embryo of her affections. She'd asked him to leave the old drama alone, but he ignored her wishes. He'd shown he wouldn't stop until he dug up every appalling detail. There remained only one way to avoid his continuous probing. She only hoped she had the courage needed to pull it off.

"I'm sorry, Jack, I don't l-love you," Ann stammered and turned away so he wouldn't see the lie in her eyes. She took a deep breath to replenish the oxygen in her bloodstream.

Her words hit Jack hard. The first woman he confessed love for had rejected him. Wouldn't half the women in Indianapolis laugh if they could see him now? "All right," he said after a long pause. "I can accept that. You may not love me now, but that doesn't mean you never can. If you'll let me hang around, I'll grow on you, I promise." He smiled at her back, needing his charm to work right now. He felt quite desperate.

"No." Ann continued shaking her head. "I'm sorry, but you'll have to abide by my decision. There's no other choice." She had difficulty holding herself together. She needed him out of the house and out of her life. "Please, leave now."

"Don't do this, Ann. Don't leave me hopeless. We can work something out if you'll only give me a chance." That sounded an awful lot like begging, even to his ears, but Jack didn't know what else he could do.

"Jack, you must go now." Ann's voice had taken on a reedy sound. She only hoped he would make a quick exit. Though it seemed to take forever, she finally heard his footsteps as he turned and started for the door. Just a few more seconds, and she could breathe again.

"You're making me pay for the way Red treated you, aren't you." Jack tried a new direction. "I'm not Red. I won't hurt you. Why did he beat you all the time, anyway?" Ann inhaled deeply, taking time to organize her thoughts.

"I'm not positive, but I think his temper started with something that happened on our wedding night."

She blushed and Jack became more intrigued than ever. "What?" he asked as he came back toward her. Her agitated hand twisted the tail of her shirt which told Jack she was disturbed. When she didn't answer immediately, he repeated the question. "What?"

"Nothing," she whispered. "Nothing happened. He couldn't." She lowered her head and her voice. "He hit me for the first time on our wedding night. After that, the violence kept growing."

Jack stopped in his tracks. That explained a lot. Now he understood why she seemed so innocent and untutored in the ways of men and women. "He never made love to you?" Jack asked, almost choking on the word love in connection with her and Red. She shook her head, and Jack mentally swaggered. "We won't have that problem, Ann. I promise you."

"Red made a lot of promises at first, too. After a couple of months, he finally stopped trying to convince me he didn't enjoy using his fists. I'm never taking a chance like that again."

"Don't think I'm giving up. I can't imagine going through life without you." Jack shot one last volley before he turned and made his exit. "I've never been in love before and now that I am, I'm going to fight for your love in return." He paused. "Just remember, you've been given notice." After that parting shot, he walked out.

The minute the door closed behind him, Ann rushed to flip the lock. She slumped against the oak panel and slid down until she sat on the floor. Burying her face in her folded arms, she wondered how she'd ended up in this situation. She'd always protected her emotions fiercely. Somehow Jack managed to slip under her guard, no doubt about it. She'd never felt like this before either, but the wonderful, terrible, gut-wrenching feeling must be love. The attraction proved too powerful to be anything else.

Ann would willingly give up anything she owned for him, even her life. The emotions were so far from anything she ever felt for Red that it would have to be measured in light years. The touch of his lips on hers set off the most incredible sensations inside, which caused the incredible sensations on her outside. Just thinking about her body's reactions to him made her blush.

Ann allowed herself a moment for reliving the wonder of his arms wrapped around her body, and then she pulled herself up from the floor and straightened her spine. She had become a strong woman. She'd lived through monstrous abuse and came out the winner. She would survive the loss of Jack's love and keep on ticking. God never promised she wouldn't have heartaches. He only promised to be with her. She could count on that.

Jack headed for the barn with a confused mind and a heavy heart. He'd believed a widow would know how to react when a man touched her passionately, but sexual pleasure had seemed so new to her and now he understood why. Nevertheless, judging by her response, she'd felt the same powerful surge of emotions he had. He possessed enough experience to know when a woman became excited by his ardor. Of course, excitement wasn't love. Her responses could have been merely sexual, but he didn't think so.

And then the reaction when he told her he loved her. Thinking back on that, he could see her gasp came from surprise and disbelief. Hadn't anyone ever said they loved her? Even though Red turned out to be a Neanderthal, surely at some point he would've at least expressed his love. But wait, he remembered someone saying her father gave her to Red. *Hmm...maybe the rattlesnake never did say he loved her. Maybe today was the first time she'd ever heard the words. Maybe she'd never been loved by anyone before.* All of a sudden, Jack's world seemed a little brighter, and it had nothing to do with Tennessee moonlight.

His step didn't seem quite so heavy by the time he entered the barn, but he wanted confirmation of his recent eye-opener, so he headed straight for Haber Judd.

"Hey, Haber, are you awake?" Jack made no attempt to keep the noise level down as he advanced on the other man.

"Ah am now," Haber Judd sighed, "'n why ya call me jist Haber? Ain't nobody ever call me that."

"Oh, sorry," Jack apologized. "Listen, I need to ask you an important question. Why did Ann marry Red...what's his real name, anyway. Surely his mother didn't name him just Red?"

"'Is name wuz Redford," Haber Judd answered as he let out another sigh. "Story went 'is mama loved 'er some Robert

Redford. She named Red after 'em." Jack thought that over and smiled.

"So why did Ann marry him," he asked again. "Surely she couldn't have been in love with the pit viper." He spit out the words like they had a bad taste.

"Ah thought Ah dun told ya. Her daddy give 'er to 'em. She did'n wanna go ta 'em, leastways not after she got ta know 'em. She mighta lacked 'em when she first saw 'em. He wuz purdy easy on the eyes."

Jack took a moment and digested that tidbit, then asked the question that burned on his mind.

Chapter 9

"They were never in love?" He held his breath. It occurred to him if Ann had never been in love, recognizing the emotion might take her a while, like it had for him. His ego remained healthy and in good working order. He refused to believe she didn't love him, too, and somehow her emotional entanglement with Red—or lack thereof—seemed important to that belief. He didn't have a long wait for the answer he coveted.

"The Mam wuz a baby, jist sebumteen, when the old geezer made 'is deal with the devil. Ah always wondered why 'e'd ruther Red ended up with 'is land than 'is own dawder. Guess 'e did'n cotton ta the Carter bunch, or may be it wuz jist the Mam's mama, Mary Sue, he did'n lack." Haber Judd paused, then continued, "Ta answer yer question, Ah don't reckon they wuz ever in love."

"I knew it!" Jack crowed, then seeing the interest on Haber Judd's face, he explained, "She seems so unused to…you know, being touched." He gave his new friend a self-conscious grimace. "That's a pretty stupid thing to say after seeing those pictures this morning, isn't it." Haber Judd studied him for a moment, and finally asked the question growing in his mind.

"Ya in love with the Mam?" the old fellow asked quietly. Jack couldn't help noticing Haber Judd's wistful expression.

"Yes, I am," he boasted. "Are my feelings that obvious?" He watched as a world-class grin spread over Haber Judd's features. That lifted his spirits tremendously. "There's a big problem though. She doesn't return my affections." All his woebegone fears were apparent in that one statement.

"Doncha be givin' up," Haber Judd yelped. "That gal never had nobody that loved 'er in 'er whole life. Gonna take a little get'n use to." Haber Judd paused and thought for a minute.

Jack could see he had something more he wanted to say, so he waited on pins and needles for Haber Judd to organize his mind.

"Ya recallect on the way ta town Ah told ya the Mam's got 'erself a powerful pride." He imparted the words as if in preparation for revealing state secrets.

Jack nodded and leaned forward, intent on catching every remark.

"Wellsir, she'd never tell ya, but she'd be feelin' a mite dim 'cause she got no ed-je-cation." Guilt for revealing her confidential information immediately consumed Haber Judd, and a hint of remorse showed in his countenance. Surprise shown on Jack's face as well.

"I don't understand," Jack said truthfully. In his sheltered life, he'd never encountered an adult without an education. "I heard her read." That statement seemed almost like a plea for a rebuttal. However, Haber Judd didn't give him one.

"She went a'nough ta learn readin' and writin'," he told his new friend, "'n she wuz good at figgerin', but even when the law said she had ta go ta school, 'er daddy kep' 'er home more'n he let 'er go. He wanted 'er around ta cook and work the garden spot—and ta beat on. Purdy soon she wuz so fer bahind she could'n cetch up. Mind ya now, she's smarter'n a whip, but they ain't no tellin' 'er that! Ah'm a thinkin' if she wuz ed-je-cated, she'd hold 'er own anywhur in this ole world!" His tone of voice might as well have said she would surely be the next president!

"I agree with you, Haber...uh...Judd," Jack said with a smile in his voice and in his heart as well. "But do you think she'll let pride interfere with our relationship?" Jack smiled bigger because he liked the idea of having a relationship with Ann. The very thought made him feel happy.

"Ah 'spect ya kin count on it."

Haber Judd answered frankly. His statement contained the truth as far as he knew, but even Haber Judd, the only human friend Ann possessed, didn't know the true extent of her reservations.

Jack thanked him for sharing those opinions. In his heart, he thanked Haber Judd for trusting him enough to reveal details he knew the older man had never told another living soul.

He and Haber Judd lay down for the night, but Jack's thoughts, ideas, and emotions kept him from closing his eyes. He had plans to make. He knew of no quick fix for the problems he faced, but he remained determined to find a solution that would be acceptable for both him and Ann. Jack spent most of the night trying to solve the many mysteries surrounding the woman of his heart, unable to sleep because he couldn't stand an unsolved puzzle.

Ann suffered through a sleepless night, too. In her life, she'd given up a great many things. She surrendered her education, not only academically, but socially, as well. Ann never had a girl friend, never dated, never learned to mix with people and that made communicating more difficult when the need arose.

Losing all those things hurt. But nothing had ever hurt this bad. Even when Red got his kicks by hitting her, she'd retained an inner strength that kept her going, kept her sane, kept her strong. She didn't feel strong at the moment. Where had that internal gumption gone? She needed a power infusion now, because she felt quite certain she faced the hardest thing she had ever tackled.

So round and round whirled the thoughts in Ann's head for the biggest part of the night. For the first time in his life, Peanut had the task of waking his mistress so she could set out his breakfast.

Because of his late night, Jack also overslept the next morning and knew he would arrive late for work. He barely managed a quick "Hi" for Ann while he wolfed down the mouthwatering breakfast she had hastily prepared. After clean up, he zipped out the door and ran straight into his father, followed by Gina Lambert.

For a moment all three people were dumbstruck, and then several things happened at once. Mike clasped Jack in a fatherly bear hug, slapping him on the back in a jovial way. Jack, coming out of a shock-induced daze, opened his mouth to ask what they were doing in Tennessee, but never got the chance. Gina threw herself at him, wrapped her arms around his neck, and planted her lips firmly on his. He became too entangled to move, or speak, as if he could do either with her body wrapped around him and her lips clamped to his. Past her head, he saw his father beaming at them.

Before he recovered his senses enough to pull away from the clinging woman who'd fastened herself on him, he saw Mike's gaze shift. Dad's smile changed from joyous to socially polite, his expression from elated to curious.

Suddenly Jack became terrified. With Gina hanging on like poison ivy, he turned. Ann stood in the doorway with her eyes glued to Gina, a look of abject horror on her face. At that sight, Jack exploded into action. He brought his hands up to grasp Gina's head and detached her mouth from his. He took hold of her shoulders and pushed her away from his body.

"Aren't you glad to see me, Darling?" Gina cooed, gazing

up at him with a sunny smile plastered on her face. "I told Dad you'd be missing me terribly by now, so he volunteered to bring me down for a visit."

Jack still stood gawking at Ann, wanting to explain that this fiasco was all a huge mistake, that Gina didn't mean spit, when his problems grew a whole lot worse.

"That's right, Son," Mike boomed. "A man shouldn't be separated from his fiancée for so long a time. Loneliness leads a man into temptation. Besides, Gina's been missing you so much. Your mother and I decided doing without your company any longer might be unhealthy for her."

Jack still stared at Ann. He watched the color leak from her face until she turned pasty white. He made a move toward her, but she turned away and rushed inside, closing the door behind her.

Gina still maintained a death grip on his arm. He hadn't yet tried to remove her when Peanut came running from the barn. The dog didn't bark. He gave out the same menacing hum he'd growled when Jack first saw him. Jack spoke his name, expecting him to change back into the friendly chum he been lately, but the big monster had taken a stand in front of the cabin door and showed no signs of moving. He didn't show any signs of being Jack's chum either.

Jack felt as if he'd been cast into a play where he had no script. Some of the spoken words were just beginning to sink into his conscious mind. *"Darling? Dad? Fiancée?"* What the fig was going on here? Even as he reviewed those words, he became aware of Gina's sexy, throaty voice.

"I hope we arrived in time to rescue you from any further embarrassment." She chuckled. "I came as soon as I could after you called."

Jack rounded on the two people who had just put a huge road block in his relationship with Ann. He intended to demand an explanation, but Peanut had other ideas. The growl became louder and more menacing. Mike and Gina were backing away. Jack turned to see Peanut crouched low with his fur standing straight up from the top of his head to the tip of his tail. He advanced toward them one slow step at a time.

"I think we'd better move on out of here," Jack told them quietly without taking his eyes off the dog. "I'll meet you at the site." In less than a minute, his visitors were inside their BMW. Jack wanted to stay and reason with Ann, and he would have, but first he had a problem that demanded his attention. He yelled he'd return later, hopped into his truck, and drove away.

Inside the house, a devastated Ann stood watching from the shadows beyond the window. Tears were not yet falling. She remained still, too wounded by the information she heard and the display she saw to move. That woman was his fiancée, and she was beautiful.

Into Ann's mind flooded the image of the woman...girl. She looked younger than Ann and taller, five foot six or seven she guessed, and she possessed equipment Ann had never even dreamed about. She had full, rounded breasts. Ann slid her palms over her chest and felt deficient. That woman had a tiny waist that flared to womanly hips. Ann couldn't find her waist under her overalls. Jack's fiancée's legs were long and shapely, making Ann's shorter ones seem stubby. The city girl had a cap of short black hair which she wore straight. Her green eyes were surrounded by a creamy, flawless complexion. A straight, regal nose sat above full, pouty lips that were painted fire engine red. As the vision formed in Ann's mind, each picture convicted her of her lack. The clothes Jack's woman wore looked like a million dollars and probably cost a small fortune. Ann barely glanced downward. She didn't need to see her clothing to know how shoddy she appeared in her father's ancient outfit.

The beauty had draped her body over Jack with such familiarity that Ann became convinced she'd performed that act many times before. She'd kissed him right in front of her. Ann felt surprise at how much that hurt. But it was the words that woman said that cut to the quick. She said Jack had called her to rescue him. From what—or whom?

She still stood in the same spot, staring into space, when Peanut gave up his sentry duty outside and came in through the doggie door. He approached her and sat at her feet looking up. When he realized he wasn't going to receive a greeting, he began licking her hand.

Then the tears came, and she began sobbing. Ann fell on her knees before the big dog and threw her arms around his neck, drenching his fur. She cried like her heart would break, because it did. Until that moment, she didn't know she'd been harboring hopes and dreams about a love affair with Jack. She had brains enough to understand she'd never have anything more with a man like him, but she believed having him in her life for a while would be enough.

She continued trying to convince herself she would settle for so little, but it proved difficult. She'd never allowed her desires to reach her conscious mind, and now that she acknowledged them, and knew they were forever out of reach, she became desolate.

Ann always believed the things she possessed were sufficient. She never wanted a man in her life, never hankered after romance, or love. She expected to live out her years with only Peanut and Haber Judd.

Now she found herself thinking of a husband, a house filled with children. *Ridiculous!* She dried her eyes. That such a thought could even enter her mind showed how far around the bend she'd gone. She must pull herself together and get back to work. Haber Judd needed her help. She'd better return to the business of earning a living instead of crying over stupid dreams that could never come true.

While Ann agonized over newly discovered fantasies, Jack prepared to face the music with his father and the barracuda who'd taken advantage of his plea for help. Oh, he had to shoulder most of the blame. If he hadn't acted like a spoiled brat and called for help from an unreliable person, he wouldn't be in this mess. If he'd acted like a man instead of a child, he wouldn't be struggling with a life altering problem.

He pulled up beside the automobile that still contained his father and the barracuda and jumped out. He came here in body, but his mind and heart were back with Ann at her house. He intended to sort this out in time to go back before she erected a brick wall around her heart. Otherwise she would build the barricade so thick he'd never be able to break it down.

As he rounded his truck and approached the BMW, his father opened the driver's door and stepped out. Gina obviously intended staying out of firing range because she made no move to exit the car.

"What's going on here, Dad?" Jack fired the first volley at the older man.

Now, Mike might be older, but he was no push-over. He narrowed his eyes and studied his son's black mood before he spoke. "Well, Son, just what you asked for, so I've been told." Mike noticed the change come over Jack's expression and knew he'd hit on something. "I take it you still want to come home?" he asked tongue in cheek. The look on Jack's face proved priceless.

"Uh, well, hmm...I...um..." Jack seemed incapable of spitting out two coherent words in a row. Taking a calming breath, he regained control of his unruly tongue. "I've decided I'll stay and see the job through, Dad."

Now that turned out to be something Mike hadn't expected. When Gina told Mike her story of their engagement and Jack inviting her to Tennessee, he knew straight away his son intended using this ploy as a means of returning home. Mike wouldn't have been surprised if he had actually married the hussy—yes, Dad knew—for the purpose of leaving the boonies and moving back to the life he loved so much.

Pressure from Jack's mother, Wilma, helped persuade Mike he should bring Gina down for a visit. He also wanted to see firsthand if working with old Dan had any effect on the boy at all. He talked with Dan on the phone, of course, but he needed to see Jack's face in order to assess the outcome. Now Jack had told him he wanted to stay and finish the job. Maybe his plan for forcing his son to grow up and be a responsible adult had worked after all.

"One might think you aren't glad to see me, Jack," Gina murmured from the other side of the car where she stood after deciding to dive into the fray. "I did come as soon as I could. I told you the arrangements would take a few days."

Jack's face turned pink. "I'm sorry, Gina, I should've called you and explained that things are different now." Jack's mind began working on a logical reason for asking her to return home as quickly as possible. Giving her the brush made him feel like a heel. After all, she had come a long way at his request.

"What's changed?" she asked as she glided around the car.

She moved as if she wore a gown in the ball room at the Marriott. How could she do that out here on this uneven ground in slacks and a jacket? Jack couldn't answer that question or hers either. And no way could he expose his fledging love in front of this woman. He turned to Mike.

"I have to stay and finish the job, and I need a favor from you. Would you take Gina home for me?"

Mike sensed a lot of undercurrents here. Before he could go home and tell Wilma he'd done his best, he must reach the bottom of Jack's latest intrigue. Convincing Mother wouldn't be that easy since he'd talked her into backing him when he sent Jack away. At least he could bring her up to date about the positive feedback from that decision.

"Tell you what, Son, let's go on back to the motel and spend the day together. You'll be able to work out an understanding with Gina, and we'll have some private time for business." Jack didn't bother thinking twice. He needed time alone with his father to acquaint him with the changes in his life—and in his heart.

"Okay, you two go ahead. I have a couple of things to discuss with Dan. After that, I'll come on over." He asked where they were staying and waved them off, then he rushed out to find Dan.

In a jiffy, he'd settled the schedule changes with his boss and left, but driving past Ann's and on to Norris took a great amount of control. Jack wanted more than a few minutes when he explained what happened this morning. All the way into town, he thought about the words he would use, and how he could say them, to make her understand. He didn't come up with a single one.

When he arrived at the motel and stepped out of his truck, he saw Gina laying in wait. Jack sighed, psychologically preparing for a confrontation.

"I'm not too happy with the reception I received this morning," she fired before he could say a word. "I came all this way on your say so. You want to put me in the picture?" Her words sounded harsh, but she walked right up to him, wrapped her arms around his neck, and planted a kiss on his mouth.

"You want to let go of me so I can tell you what happened?" Jack had the air of a doomed man.

Gina only shook her head. "I like it right where I am," she purred. "And you did offer yourself up on the altar of my lust for just a teensy weensy favor. I've delivered the favor. It's time for you to pay up."

She looked at him with the eyes of Eve. They smoldered with a carnal knowledge that left him sweating. She was just a girl, only eighteen years old. How had she become so worldly?

"Look, Gina, I'm sorry about this." Jack made an effort to hold himself away from the clutching creature whose tentacles had an iron tight grip around his neck. "If you'll give me a little space, I'll try and explain." He reached up and gripped her wrists, pulling them down from his shoulders, but the minute he let go, they were right back up there. "Come on, Gina," he growled.

"Oh, I'd love to," she growled right back.

This was a pickle. Jack had begun thinking on another approach when a movement caught his eye. He looked beyond the girl/woman who had a stranglehold on him and directly into the eyes of Deke Hendricks. He moaned.

He expected the big man would make some snide remark, but Deke turned in the other direction and walked away. Jack knew what that meant. He knew exactly what the man thought, the same thing any other man would think, the same thing Jack himself would think if the situations were reversed, that he had a clandestine meeting with—he looked down at Gina's upturned face—with a young, more than willing woman. He pushed her away with enough force to detach her from his person. Looking at her youth made him feel like a dirty old man.

"Listen, there's been a mistake." Jack almost yelled. He watched her eyes narrow and knew he had made the mistake by inviting her here, and the blunder had grown into a big one. "Please, try to understand. Things have changed since I called you. I should've let you know, but I've been so busy I forgot." Uh oh. Wrong thing to say.

"You *forgot!*" Gina shouted. Her face screwed up in rage, her eyes turned red, and he felt certain he saw smoke coming from her ears. "*You forgot!*" The fuming woman bellowed, seemingly unable to make it past those two words.

"I'm really sorry." Jack tried to do damage control. "I'm a pig, I know, but I didn't forget on purpose. Let me make it up to you. I'll buy you that diamond bracelet you admired the time we flew to New York." He gave her his most effective little-boy-lost look. It didn't work.

"Yes, you will," she said and Jack thought he might have hit on something that would dig him out of this jam. "We'll talk about the bracelet later," she told him as she turned away.

Jack didn't feel quite as confident that his troubles were over. Something about the way she said those words sounded wrong. He couldn't put his finger on the threat exactly, but he had a gut feeling he'd just made a dangerous enemy.

"There you are, Son. Come on inside." Mike beckoned from a doorway only a few feet behind Jack. Jack spun around, wondering how much of that conversation his father heard. He hung his head and followed Dad into his room.

The unit seemed nice enough with two full beds, a dresser and a TV, but it looked like most rooms in the less luxurious motel chains. That was one advantage about the resort they were putting up. Their establishment would be an alternative from the more generic choices. This kind of motel served a good purpose, but right now this area presented few options for the relaxation of weary travelers. He suddenly felt proud to be a part of his family's company, and of his connection with his father's business. He discovered yet another satisfaction he'd never felt before.

"Well, Jack, have I been bamboozled?" Mike asked his firstborn. He studied his twenty-nine year old son and thought he detected a change. Jack didn't look sullen and angry as he had the last time they stood face to face. Even when he bowed his head, Mike thought he stood prouder than he ever had before. He hoped the observation wasn't wishful thinking on his part.

"I'm sorry, Dad." Jack began the same way he had with Gina. "I should have put a stop to this charade before the drama reached this point."

Jack sighed. Mike sensed a confession coming up. He wanted to help. "Let's sit down and you can tell me all about the arrangement." With that suggestion, he waved his progeny into one of the chairs and Jack complied. When they were both seated, he began again.

"You were right, Dad, but not about everything. I had started drinking too much, but I never became involved in drugs. I didn't stray that far, thank God. And I pretty much treated all the women I knew like playthings. I didn't even realize what I had done until after you had your talk with me and banished me to Tennessee. But I didn't seduce Gina. The harassment worked the other way around. She chased me everywhere. I finally gave in to her demands from sheer exhaustion and with hopes of getting rid of her." At this point, Jack stopped and took a breath, assessing the effect of his words.

Mike decided he would insert a question while he had the chance. "Did you ask her to come down here?"

Jack gulped. The time for truth had come, but the words stuck in his throat. He cleared the blockage and took the proverbial bull by the horns. "Yes, I did, right after I arrived. I was still hopping mad and willing to do anything in order to escape my exile." Jack wiped his brow. "I'd already called everyone else I knew and found out I didn't have any real friends. Gina was my last hope."

Mike had watched Jack closely, and his son's face held sincerity. Still, he believed bringing everything out in the open would be a good idea. "How do you feel about her now?" Mike didn't really need words to inform him that Jack had changed his mind about the lengths he would go to for a ticket home. The look on Jack's face told him all he needed to know. He let his son speak the words anyway, thinking the boy might need to hear them for his own edification.

"I haven't changed my mind about her. She's a brazen little baggage, and I can't tell you how much I regret having asked for her help." Jack looked his father in the eye. "I've made a lot of mistakes in the last few years, but I don't mind admitting this one is the top dog." Mike nodded in agreement, which surprised Jack. He thought his father would rake him over the coals for leading the young daughter of a client down the garden path. Goes to show.

"I'm glad to hear you say that, Son." Mike didn't hesitate in revealing his pleasure. "I knew that girl would be trouble the minute I laid eyes on her, but I doubted you knew. When she started making all that noise about a marriage between the two of you, I recognized the necessity of shipping you out of harm's way, even if you did deserve what she threatened." Mike sighed. "That wasn't the only reason, though. I believed you needed to learn appreciation for the blessings you've been handed. Did I do wrong?"

Jack smiled. "You're a wily old fox. Dan was just the man to take some of that young starch out of a wet-behind-the-ears kid with an attitude." He reached across the table and grasped his father's arm. "Thanks, Dad." Moisture formed in Mike's eyes, and he smiled at his beloved son.

"Thank you for being wise enough to learn from a man with a lot less education than you," Mike told him. "And thanks for being man enough to admit when you've made a mistake. Now, tell me about the woman in the overalls."

Chapter 10

"That's Ann Mason," Jack said, not really sure how else to start, but beaming because of parental approval. Jack became eager to tell his Dad about the new—the only—woman in his life.

"She's the one I told you about. You know, the lady one of our employees tried courting in order to obtain her signature on an agreement so we could buy her land." Jack gave his sire a knowing look.

Mike raised his eyebrows. He hadn't forgotten about the telephone conversation with Jack that had, at first, raised his and Wilma's anticipation. They hoped their son had formed a serious attachment to someone of the female persuasion. That hopefulness existed only until he talked with the front men who'd been in Tennessee and spoken directly with Ann. What they told him created doubts. Would an uneducated farm girl like her jump at the chance to hook up with a wealthy kid from the city?

"That little scrap of humanity is the one who held off all my men?" he asked Jack with a great deal of faked surprise and dry humor. "Maybe we should hire her as a front man." They laughed, but they both recognized the action as a delaying tactic. Mike settled down and waited for his son to move on to the meat of the matter.

"I love her, Dad." Jack finally spoke the words Mike dreaded hearing. He nodded, indicating that he understood. Now that the admission lay out in the open, words started pouring from the younger of the two men.

"She's the most honest person I've ever known. I can't wait for you to meet her, I mean properly. You'll love her." Jack's expression turned sober. "She's suffered a hard life, and I have a long way to go in winning her trust. This morning didn't help a bit. That's one of the reasons I must stay here, Dad, but not the only reason. I really want to finish this project."

Jack couldn't have said anything Mike would've enjoyed hearing more if he'd talked all day, but the older man had mountains of reservations about this young woman who'd caught his son's fancy.

"I take it you're serious about this Ann person." Mike's concern gave him courage to ask. "I mean, are we talking a living together kind of arrangement here?" Mike's tone of voice became just a tad too hopeful.

Jack didn't have to think twice about the best way of answering that question. Only one reply existed. "A permanent kind of arrangement, Dad. I mean to marry her, if she'll have me."

Well, that sure answered the question, thought Mike as he grew worried. He became relieved that he'd brought Gina with him.

"Are you sure you know her well enough to make a decision like that?" Mike broke out in a sweat. "I mean you've only been in Tennessee a little over a month. You don't want to rush the life-long choice of a wife." The look on Jack's face told him he wasted his breath.

"I don't need more time to know how I feel about Ann. The only thing I need time for is convincing her she feels the same way about me."

Jack's sober expression had taken on a tinge of sadness. Mike didn't want to see his son hurt. Nevertheless, he felt tremendously comforted. "She doesn't love you?" he asked Jack, not realizing his relief showed. "Maybe she doesn't know what a good catch you are. If you tell her you're one of the richest young men in Indianapolis, maybe she'll fall instantly in love with you."

Mike's sarcasm didn't go over Jack's head. He sprang to his feet at once. "You don't know her at all," he shouted. "Maybe you don't know me, either. You come riding to the rescue, bringing that female octopus with you, and you proceed to tell me what's best for me. For once in my life, I know what's best for me. Ann is. I'm telling you here and now, if I can't convince her to come home with me, I won't be coming home at all." Having delivered that declaration, Jack headed straight for the exit, rammed through the opening, and slammed the door shut before Mike could shift himself into first gear.

That went well, Mike mused.

In the room next to his, a pair of green cat eyes glittered with malice. *So, a female octopus, am I?* She wasn't good enough for one of the richest young man in Indianapolis? Gina seethed with rage. So the brat thought he could get away with treating her like this? She would show him. He didn't know who he messed with, but he was about to find out. *Just you wait, Jackson Barrister, just you wait.*

Jack had grown so incensed he drove right past Ann's house and had to turn around and go back. Of all the nerve. Didn't the old man hear a word he said? Where were all those morals he'd shot at Jack back in his office in Indianapolis? Jack told his dad he loved Ann, and Mike suggested they live together? Jack was totally teed off.

When he arrived back at Ann's house and turned into the driveway, he noticed the police car sitting there. Or, to be more precise, the sheriff's Oldsmobile. Jack immediately remembered meeting Deke's eyes over Gina's head. Trouble.

He parked the Hummer, climbed out, and walked toward the house. As he approached the back door that led into the kitchen, he heard Deke's voice speaking loudly.

"Why do you set yourself up for these things?" His question echoed slightly quieter than the Concord.

A low feminine voice murmured in response, and Jack's insides clinched in knots. He couldn't distinguish the words, but he knew the voice belonged to Ann.

Jack rushed the door with the intention of putting a stop to their conversation. Deke might cause irreparable damage to Jack's chances of mending the wall of misunderstandings built between him and Ann.

He exploded through the opening and found Ann and Deke standing less than three feet apart, facing each other. They both turned toward him, their expressions equally shocked to see him standing in the doorway. Neither one looked pleased to see him.

Sheriff Hendricks bristled. He seemed to swell another inch upward, making him look roughly the size of a grizzly. He took a step toward the smaller man, but Ann put a restraining hand on his arm.

"Don't, Deke. Please," Ann pleaded with the mountain.

Deke looked down at the small hand lying on his massive arm, and Jack could've sworn he saw the big man wilt. Then Deke lifted his eyes to hers, and in that instant Jack knew he wasn't the only one in love with Ann.

Anesthetized to the fact that the other man could break him in two, Jack moved toward Ann as fast as his legs would carry him. He reached her side in three steps and circled her waist with his arm. He glowered at Deke over her head, staking his claim. He took a step backward, hauling Ann with him, thereby detaching her hand from Deke's arm.

She looked up at him in surprise and began forming an objection because of his misguided presumption, but one glance told her he stood ready to fight Deke. She looked back at Deke, then at Jack, and then back at Deke. The man must be crazy! Deke would make mincemeat out of him!

She looked at Jack again. Strangely, she had no fear of him. Here she stood, held against a man in a towering rage, and she didn't feel the least bit afraid. What a revelation! She took one second for relishing that eye-opener before she put an end to the standoff.

"Stop this right now." She quietly pried Jack's hands loose and stepped out of his reach. "Deke, I want you to leave. Please," she added, softening the command. "I must speak with Jack in private." Deke eyed Jack for a bit, gave Ann a penetrating look, nodded and turned to go. He paused at the doorway and told her she need only call if she wanted him. Next, giving Jack another dirty look, he walked out of the house, lumbered into his car, and drove away.

With the sheriff gone, a hush settled over the room. Neither of the remaining two people knew quite how to proceed. In the uneasy atmosphere, Peanut made his presence known by prancing from one to the other, nudging them, and licking their hands. On his second pass, Jack knelt to reassure the big dog and give him a cuddle. Ann started making busy work by folding the dish cloth and kitchen towels, which she immediately unfolded and used for wiping the table, the cabinet, the stove.

"Let's talk," Jack said, rising from the floor and moving toward her. She halted his progress by holding her palm out at him. He stopped and began his explanation. "I'm not engaged to Gina. I never have been." Jack took a breath, preparing to continue, except she butted in.

"Your father seems to think you are." Ann tamped down the hurt in her voice. "And that girl looked right at home in your arms. Are you telling me she's never been there before?"

Jack began sweating egg-sized pellets. What a loaded question.

"Aargh." He coughed to clear the blockage from his throat. "I dated her briefly before I came here, but the fling had fizzled by the time I left Indiana." Judging by the look on her face, Jack didn't think he'd made any headway.

"So you didn't ask her to come and rescue you?" The question seemed rhetorical, but he tried giving an answer anyway.

"When I first came here, I felt very angry with my father. He'd ordered me to Tennessee against my will." Saying these words to Ann measured far beyond difficult. Jack swallowed his male pride, allowing the woman he loved to see he'd been a bad son. "I tried contacting several people I believed I could count on for assistance, but they wouldn't even return my calls. Gina was the only one willing to offer help. I thought if I could just go home, everything would be all right." He took another step toward her.

"I don't know, Jack, for a father who'd banished his son

from his home and a woman who'd been dumped, they both looked awfully glad to see you. Especially Gina, isn't that the name you called her?" Ann adapted an innocent look. "You didn't introduce us." All that innocence disappeared in a flash. "I wonder why?"

Jack knew hot water when he felt boiling liquid rising up around his neck. All his life, he'd dealt with people who were eager to do his bidding, who wanted to make him happy. Even his father, and especially his mother, always wanted only the best for him. When he disagreed with what they thought best, they always caved in, until the last time when they sent him south. He'd never recognized the fact, but he had become a spoiled brat. All that catering to his ego left him ill-equipped for negotiating with a hostile opponent.

"I'm sorry, I acted rudely," he began, feeling as if he waded through molasses. "I felt so shocked at seeing Dad and Gina here, I couldn't think straight."

Ann struggled to keep all emotion from her expression. She didn't want him knowing he'd broken her heart. She knew, as she had even before the appearance of his visitors, that she must force him out of her life. Ann didn't believe Jack could have lasting feelings for her anyway. She felt certain his interest proved only that he had a strong case of lust.

"I couldn't care less about your lack of manners," she sighed. "I just wondered why you felt the need for a rescue squad." Jack took another step and Ann finally realized just how close he'd come, but evasive tactics proved too late because he reached out, took hold of her shoulders, and pulled her against his chest. He wrapped his arms around her and put his lips against her ear.

"You listen to me," he whispered. "You're the only woman I want." When he sucked her lobe into his mouth and tasted her, she thought she might faint. "Since the first time I saw you, I couldn't stop thinking about you. I love you. I want to marry you, Ann." He breathed her name into her ear and kissed her there.

Ann shivered with the thrills of excitement he created. The hands she had lifted to push him away were now unfurled and sliding up his chest, caressing instead of pushing. Her legs turned to jelly, her stomach fluttered with the ever-present herd of butterflies. How could he unleash such passion with just a touch?

Jack felt the response of her body and his heart rejoiced. He slid his lips across her cheek and, with their bodies touching from knees to neck, he melded their mouths together. *Bliss!*

Ann had no experience at love making because she'd never indulged in the pleasure until Jack came along, but she learned fast. She wrapped her arms around his neck and kissed him right back. As her body entwined with his, her heart began unfolding from the rigid control she'd imposed upon it all her life. Light flooded into the dark place inside where she hid her emotions from the hurts inflicted by other men. Love opened into full bloom.

Ann had never known such freedom. Chains broke from around the vault where her heart had always dwelt, and sunshine poured into her soul. Love and freedom were side by side with the physical pleasure she undoubtedly felt with Jack. She couldn't differentiate one from the other.

They were all the same.

The two lovers were so lost in each other that neither became aware of a third presence until they heard the door slam and the hum of a non-threatening growl. They jerked apart and looked in the direction of the quickly fading noise. There they encountered flashing green eyes.

"Well, well, well, what have we here? I see you're up to your old tricks, Jack," Gina said. The venom spewed from lips painted bright red and curled with cruelty. "Have you got her into bed with your pretty lies yet? Or is she smarter than me. Have you told her you love her?" Those glittering, cold green eyes turned upon Ann. "He will, you know. He'll say anything to persuade a woman to sleep with him at least once, then its goodbye Charlie. I speak from experience. Has he made you feel alive, turned on the sunshine, made you feel you could trust him with your life, your heart? Has he asked you to marry him?"

"Shut up," Jack shouted. He grew so frightened he couldn't suck in air. He had to find a way of stopping Gina before she ruined his life. He moved toward her, but her rescue came from a surprising source. Peanut suddenly stood between him and Gina, issuing an uncertain growl. The poor dog had been trained from puppy-hood to protect the smaller from the larger until doing that became second nature. But, though Gina looked smaller, he certainly recognized Jack as his friend. The dog became very confused.

Join the club, thought Ann. She didn't like this stranger who came charging into her home making accusations, but the tale she told sure rang true. Jack had been sweeping Ann off her feet. He'd told her he loved her and tried to make love with her. This Gina person seemed to look inside her and see all the emotions Jack made her feel. Gina surely must have felt those same emotions with him at some point if she could describe them so perfectly.

Jack stood glaring at the girl. Ann wondered if his rage grew because Gina might be ruining his seduction plans. She felt sick and terrified. Ann forced her vulnerable, hurting heart back into the vault it had recently escaped and replaced the chains, tightening them painfully around the poor prisoner. She clanged the door shut, leaving her emotions in the darkness to which they were accustomed. The love-bloom folded and caution regained control.

"Get out," she hissed, "both of you, get out!" Jack whirled around, belatedly noticing the results of Gina's work.

"Ann, don't let her drive a wedge between us," he cried. "That's exactly what she set out to do. Don't let her succeed. I love you!"

Gina laughed an evil laugh. "And this morning at the motel you were loving me," the wicked girl screeched. "He'll probably tell you he spent all that time with Mike, but, Honey, I'm here to tell you I look nothing like his dad."

Jack started toward Ann with his hand extended, but she called Peanut to come and guard. The poor confused dog did as she commanded, though anyone could see his heart wasn't in the job. He barely growled.

Ann looked at Jack with eyes full of suspicion. She remembered what sheriff Hendricks told her about seeing Jack and Gina in a clinch outside a motel door. That's why he'd come today. He warned her not to let Jack hurt her. He told her that because of what he'd seen, he feared Jack might be stringing her along. Evidently he'd been right.

"Get out," Ann whispered again, and Peanut finally snapped to full attention.

Gina, seeing a real threat from the dog, and feeling she'd done a good job of revenging herself on Jack, made a hasty exit. The unrepentant she-devil left him to face the music she'd started conducting.

"Ann, you must listen," he began. "That girl is an evil person. She's out to cause trouble, and she's good at it." He didn't intend to stop talking until he'd told her everything. He paused only once to take a breath. That's when she let go with a gut shot.

"Deke told me he saw you kissing her this morning," she stated, deliberately keeping her voice calm and level. "Is that true?"

What could he say? Jack had been caught in a web woven

by an expert, a black, poisonous spider. No matter how he answered, losing seemed the most likely conclusion. Perhaps the time had come for a counterattack.

"I'll answer your question if you'll answer mine." Jack narrowed his eyes. "Did you kill your husband?" He immediately felt ashamed of his bluntness. Her eyes grew as big as half dollar's, and her face turned as white as Aunt Lillie's hair. She actually stumbled backward a step as if he'd hit her.

"How dare you!" Ann said in true heroine fashion.

Jack might have smiled under other circumstances, but he couldn't find any humor in anything at the moment. "I dare because it's time you trust me enough to tell the truth. I know there's more to the story than what I've heard so far." He ran his fingers through his hair, mussing the strands even more than the turbulent morning had already done. "I'm on your side. Tell me!"

Her face darkened as color returned with a vengeance. She cast her eyes toward the floor. "That's none of your business," she muttered, knowing she must now sever the ties. Without meeting his eyes, she said the hardest words she'd ever uttered. "Now go home, and I mean back to Indiana. I want you out of my life." In spite of her broken heart, her voice emerged strong and definite.

Jack felt frustrated and angry. He wanted to shake her, but even if he were actually willing to commit violence against Ann, Peanut would surely rip him to shreds. Words were the only weapons he possessed.

"I'm not staying around and begging for affection from a woman who doesn't trust me with her secrets. If a relationship has any chance of succeeding, the people involved must share their hearts. Not just the good things, but the bad things, too. I'll be the first to tell you I'm far from perfect, but you made me want to be. Let me make the attempt with you." He just couldn't help trying one more time.

Oh, how she wanted to fall into his arms and say yes, yes, yes! But that option remained unavailable for her. Jack was a very determined man. She could see that. He wouldn't stop picking at her until she told him everything he wanted to know. The temptation became almost overwhelming. Even now, she wanted to tell him all her secrets and be done with the deception. How long would she last if he picked at her every day? Impossible.

And that didn't even take into account the painted lady he shared an engagement with. Maybe the woman was lying, or maybe not. She wanted to believe Gina lied, but some of her story sounded too much like Ann's relationship with Jack. How could Ann be sure? True or false, it didn't matter anyway. Even if her explanation turned out to be a sham, Ann couldn't have Jack for herself. She had to face the finish, cut him out of her life, and be done with the yearning.

"I said get out," she repeated. Saying those words took every bit of her strength and courage, and if he didn't go soon she would throw herself into his arms and pour out her love. She had to make him leave. "Go now, or you'll force me to release Peanut."

Jack felt so many emotions, but the minute she threatened him with Peanut, the most prominent one became rage. "You got it, Mam," he mocked Haber Judd's name for her, "and don't expect to see me again. I won't be back." He had begun shouting before he'd made it half way through the speech, and had gone out the door by the time he finished. He met up with Haber Judd outside and sprinted right past him like a thoroughbred racehorse headed for the finish line.

"Hold yer horses, Jack," Haber Judd called after him as he ran to catch up. They were inside the barn before the old man came close enough to talk. "Whut's goin' on?" he asked, out of breath and completely mystified.

"Your Mam just kicked me off her place." Jack practically spat the words at Haber Judd. "And I've decided that's the best idea she's had in a long time." He continued grabbing his belongings as fast as he could. He didn't have much. He sure wouldn't take the clothes she'd given him. He turned and rushed out the door, running from this place—and the hurt Ann had inflicted—as fast as he could. He anger simmered too hot for anything else.

"Jack, wait up." Haber Judd huffed as he hurried to catch the younger man before he escaped. He moved close enough to grab Jack's arm, and then he held on, gulping in air. "Ya kin't jist walk away lack this. Ya told the Mam ya love 'er."

"How I feel doesn't matter, Haber Judd. She doesn't love me. She told me so, and she proved it by refusing to share the truth. I don't have a choice. I have to go." And that was that. Haber Judd let go of his arm and he left.

The old man hurried into the house to check on Ann. He feared she would surely be smarting. He found her standing in front of the window watching Jack drive away, and waited until the truck drove out of sight before he spoke.

"Mam, why'd jue let 'em go?" Haber Judd asked the unhappy young woman who stood with her back toward him. She sighed and turned to face her old friend.

"It's for the best, Haber Judd." Her answer sounded as sad as she looked. "I'm sure he would have grown tired of me before long. This way, the affair is over before it begins and I can start healing now. He has another woman waiting in Norris. She's someone he can take home to meet his mom and dad. Even if he'd been serious about a relationship with me, which I doubt, can't you just see me in some rich man's house wearing fancy clothes, drinking champagne, and eating caviar?" She laughed, but the chuckle sounded hollow and false.

"Yez Mam, Ah sure kin see ya that a way." Haber Judd answered just as if she expected a reply. "Ah'm thinkin' ya'd be a grand lady anywhur ya went, and Jack'd be lucky ta have ya. Ya should'a stopped 'em, Mam, 'e did'n wanna go." Ann's face fell even farther.

"I couldn't let him stay, Haber Judd," she cried softly. "He just wouldn't stop picking. He meant to get to the bottom of Red's death. You know I can't let that happen." She began crying in earnest.

Haber Judd felt about as low as a snake's belly. He stepped closer and patted her shoulder. Haber Judd touching anyone in sympathy rarely happened, especially a woman, especially a white woman, so Ann valued his attempt to reassure her. She felt humbled that he cared so much, but his compassion didn't make the hurt go away.

* * * *

Jack headed for the building site in order to try and catch up with Dan. Even though the hour grew late and most of the workers would be gone, he thought he'd find Dan still there. He needed a one-on-one with his boss before he left. In spite of what his father thought, he couldn't walk away from this job without Dan's consent.

He found Dan going over the next day's schedule with a crew manager. Jack requested a minute of his time and Dan dismissed the other man, telling Jack they were through anyway. In less than five minutes, Jack had explained his need to go home and told Dan he would call in a few days. The older man approved the time off, and Jack started on his way again.

He stopped where the resort marina would be when they completed the project. The area contained little more than a dock now. He sat without purpose, letting random thoughts run through his mind. He'd read a lot about the area since he came to Tennessee. At this moment and in this place, he could be sitting in the same spot Daniel Boone and Davy Crockett had sat. They had undoubtedly looked at this very same valley—without the lake—after they traveled the Cumberland Gap.

Though awe-inspiring, that piece of history proved insufficient to take his mind off his monumental problems for any length of time. His worries came flooding back to take control of his consciousness without any invitation from him.

This was the same place where he sat looking out over the lake...just last night? Incredible! He couldn't believe so many major changes had occurred in less than twenty-four hours, turbulent hours that had torn apart a life he'd only begun to hope for.

He tried to find peace and calm in watching the water, but the effects didn't last any longer this evening than it had the night before. He started the engine and drove away.

Chapter 11

In his truck, headed for Norris, Jack's mind turned over the things he'd uncovered since he came to Tennessee. Ordinarily he had no problem organizing his thought processes, but today his seething emotions blocked the way and turned his gray matter into a jumbled mess.

When he tried to work out the puzzle of Ann, his brain wouldn't co-operate. Too many pieces of information whirled around inside his head and too many were missing for an easy, sensible solution. But he would solve the mystery, eventually, if for no other reason than he couldn't stand an unsolved puzzle.

One thing remained certain. Jack lied when he told Ann he wouldn't be back. He couldn't give up on the first woman he'd ever loved. He needed a few brain-organizing days away without the stress of dealing with the stubborn love of his life. He smiled inwardly. Boy, was she in for a surprise.

Jack arrived back at the motel where his father rented a room. Mike had obviously been watching for him. He came out before Jack cut the engine and stood by the truck waiting for him to open the door.

"I'm sorry, Son," Mike said as soon as Jack could hear. "I was out of line. Your love life is none of my business."

Jack straightened and stood facing his Dad in the wedge created between the truck and the open door. "It's a dead issue." Bittersweetness coated Jack's every word. "Ann proved you were so completely wrong about her. She turned me down." The bitterness existed because his father had tried to manage his life. The sweetness came because Mike realized he'd acted wrongly and didn't mind admitting his mistake.

"I'm sorry, Jack," Mike repeated with a great amount of astonishment and real regret. "I'll go out and talk to her, if you want. I can explain what happened, why I brought Gina with me." Mike's amazement increased. He couldn't imagine a woman existed in the world that would turn Jack down. Evidently his son had proved very astute at recognizing true merit in the fairer sex, in spite of a few false starts. Mike's chest puffed out with parental pride.

"That won't be necessary. I've had all the help I can stand for one day. Gina came out and gave Ann her version of the reason for your visit." Jack looked toward the closed door beside his father's unit. "Where is the pit viper anyhow?"

"She left about an hour ago," Mike estimated. "She didn't say a word to me. She hired a car and took off, I assumed for the airport because she took all her bags. Can't say it bothered me too much. How did someone so young become so mean?"

Jack just shook his head. He didn't know the answer either.

He gave his father an edited version of his parting from Ann and told him he intended going home for a visit. He quickly explained he'd already squared everything with Dan. Mike asked if he had equally squared everything with Ann. Jack admitted he left because he couldn't figure out a way to accomplish that at the moment.

Another reason for going was the fear of doing irreparable damage to his cause if he stayed where he had access to Ann. He needed time away to regroup and come up with a better strategy.

Father and son ambled to the motel restaurant and spent the next thirty minutes making plans for their departure. They ordered a couple of burgers and some fries, wolfed them down, and returned to Mike's room. Jack stretched out on the extra bed and, because of his wakefulness the night before, fell instantly asleep.

Early the next morning, they set out for Indiana—Mike in his BMW, and Jack in the Hummer. Neither felt any interest in having breakfast quite that soon, so they agreed they would drive for an hour or so before stopping to eat. As they headed north on Interstate 75, the beautiful rolling hills of northeastern Tennessee leveled to lush, gentle swells.

They'd crossed the state line into Kentucky when Mike, who had taken the lead, spotted a likely restaurant and pulled off the interstate. The eatery looked clean and tidy nestled by a small lake surrounded by oaks and ash. The spot created an oasis perfect for the relaxation of weary travelers. Jack and Mike strolled inside and took a seat.

The main dining area had been decorated in regional memorabilia from the distant past. The walls were hung with pictures of old cars, people from the area dressed in clothing long out of style, and old southern farms. A picture of federal marshals busting up a distillery took pride of place. Most of the photographs depicted common folk instead of the more wealthy elite.

Mike and Jack ordered a hearty breakfast, and while they waited for their food, Jack told his Dad about the wonderful meals Ann prepared for him.

"Once I persuade her to marry me, I'll become as fat as the neighbor's pig." He laughed. Gazing around the room as his merriment faded, his eyes passed over a nearby picture and slid right back.

Jack stopped his chitchat in the middle of a sentence. He studied the photograph a moment before he stood and rushed over for a better look. At the sight he saw, ideas formed inside his head. Concepts that previously wouldn't have occurred burst into life. He approached the counter, asked a few questions, and had a nice talk with the long-time owner.

A very excited Jack returned to the table where a mystified Mike waited for him. The younger man sat down and began explaining what had just happened.

Jack became almost too keyed up for eating breakfast, but

he forced himself to sit and eat every bite on his plate. After that exercise in discipline, he said goodbye to his father, climbed in the Hummer, and headed back the way he came, leaving the bill for Mike.

At mid-morning, Jack pulled into the drive in front of Ann's house. A second later, Peanut raced around the corner with a wagging tail and a big doggie smile on his excited face. Well, at least one of the inhabitants here looked happy to see him.

He climbed down from of the Hummer, received his greeting from the lovable brute, and started in the direction the dog had come from, knowing Peanut would have been with Ann.

He rounded the corner of the house and there she stood. She had dressed as usual in her overalls, checked work shirt, old felt hat and gumboots. She was the most beautiful thing he'd ever seen. And she had her shotgun pointed at his chest.

"Going to shoot me, Ann?" he murmured. "I know you're a murderess, but are you sure you have the guts to do it again?" Jack knew he communicated pure meanness. He watched as her face drained of all color before he walked toward her one slow step at a time. He wrapped his hand around the barrels of the shotgun, and pressed the business end against his chest. "Well, what are you waiting for? Go ahead, pull the trigger." Tears welled in her sky blue eyes and fell over the edge of already red rims to roll down her cheeks.

Jack felt like the nastiest piece of work on earth, but he

was fighting for his future and he would fight dirty if he must. She'd forced him to do just that. "Come on, don't be shy. Haber Judd's right over there, watching. He'll back you up when the police come, won't you, Haber Judd?" Jack didn't take his eyes off Ann's face, but he knew Haber Judd hadn't moved an inch since he'd come around the corner of the house.

"Mam, best put that gun down," Haber Judd said carefully. "He knows ya ain't gonna shoot 'em." Jack looked over at Haber Judd for the first time since he returned.

"Now, how would I know that, Haber Judd?" Jack practically sneered. "After all, she's already killed one man. What's one more?" A startled cry from Ann brought his attention back to her. "You don't mind me saying it, do you? Everyone in Anderson County already believes you murdered Red, so what difference does it make if I say the words out loud?" He took a deep breath and yelled at the top of his lungs. "Ann Mason is a murderer!"

By now, Ann sobbed hysterically, Peanut growled with malicious intent, and Haber Judd stood six inches from his nose. Haber Judd's hand shot out like a bullet and grabbed the gun from both Ann and Jack. In a flash, the weapon pointed at Jack's chest once again, only this time he wasn't so sure the trigger wouldn't be pulled.

"You git!" Haber Judd ordered. This man had become a Haber Judd Jack had never seen. He looked about twelve feet tall and as wide as the Hummer with that shotgun in his hands, and Jack imagined his eyes were blood red. A fire burned in the old man all right. Any threat to Ann clearly brought about a personality change in the otherwise agreeable human being.

Now he had a rip-roaring mad Haber Judd on his left side, a snarling, growling, man-eating monster at his belly button, and a frantic woman just beyond the dog. He thought retreat sounded like a good idea. He relaxed his stance as much as his tense muscles would allow, crossed his arms, and put a finger to his chin.

"Do we have a problem here?" he asked as innocently as a six day old baby. "Such a show of force over a true statement. Tut, tut." Jack furrowed his brow and narrowed his eyes in an attempt to look mean and unafraid. He possessed neither trait, but he must make them believe he did if this bluff had any chance of succeeding.

"Just leave," Ann cried.

Jack's resolve almost melted. He stiffened his backbone and looked her right in the eye. "I'm not going anywhere."

Ann knew she should be troubled by the frank statement, but her poor imprisoned heart couldn't manage truly wishing him gone. "What do you want from me?" she cried. World War Three had just broken out inside Ann. Her heart battled with her head. She had become the only casualty—so far. She needed to make sure that stayed true. She couldn't let Haber Judd be a victim of her circumstances, too.

"I want what I've always wanted—you, in bed, under me." Jack proceeded, trying to shock her further. "That's what you think, isn't it? Oh, and the truth might be nice." With those words he turned his glare back on Haber Judd. "You have anything to say, Haber Judd?" Jack's eyes bore into the old man's until the fire died out and he bowed his head.

At that moment, Ann knew for certain that she and Haber Judd had a *big* problem. "Don't say a word, Haber Judd," she screamed.

At her shrill, panicky tone, Peanut jumped forward and clamped his mouth around Jack's arm. He obviously still considered Jack a friend because he didn't sink his teeth into the flesh, but the threat was implied.

The dog's action produced immediate results. Jack froze. Haber Judd dropped the gun and reached for Peanut's collar. Ann sprang forward, shouting for Peanut to heel, sit, stay, any command that did not motivate chewing.

Within seconds the poor confused animal was pulled from Jack and incarcerated by arms and legs and hands of the humans he loved most. Jack heaved a sigh of relief.

"It's okay, Peanut. You're a good dog. You don't need to protect your mistress from me, though." Jack stood looking into Ann's tear drenched eyes. "I would never hurt her. I love her as much as you do." Jack looked at the old man who remained tangled up with the other two. "And you don't have to protect her from me, either." He looked back at Ann. "And you don't have to protect Haber Judd from me, Darling Ann. I have no intention of harming a kinky hair on his head."

For just a moment, time stood still in Ann's heart. Could

he be saying what she thought? She slowly rose from the pile of flesh and fur, looking into his eyes the whole time. Hope became a living organism inside her.

"I don't understand," she said cautiously, still afraid to believe in the miracle Jack offered.

"Could we go in the house?" he sighed. "I think I need to sit down."

"Are you hurt? Did Peanut bite your arm? Let me see." Ann stood at his side in an instant, running her hands over his arm and squealing with fear when she discovered a wet spot. She felt vastly relieved when she realized the moisture was only doggie slobber.

Ann led Jack inside and fussed over him, bringing a wet cloth, a cold drink, and a pillow for his back. Finally he demanded she sit down so they could talk, and she reluctantly took a chair.

"The time has come, Ann," he began. "I need the truth from you." He waited. And waited. The look on her face told Jack bushels. His heart pounded with the fear that maybe he'd been wrong. Maybe Ann didn't have passionate feelings for him at all. Maybe the love thing had grown from self-delusion on his part.

"I wish I could give you what you want, Jack," she finally spoke, hesitantly. "I really do, but I can't." At her statement she watched Jack deflate. She truly did want to tell him everything. Unburdening herself would be such a relief, but she had sworn she would never reveal the events of that night, sworn to herself, a vow she would not, could not, break. She felt those damnable tears saturating her eyes again.

"Listen to me, Ann," Jack demanded in a fierce voice. "The first time I heard an account of the death of Red Mason, I knew something sounded wrong. The story didn't make sense, but I couldn't put my finger on the problem. You wouldn't help me solve the mystery, even Haber Judd clammed up when I probed too much. Then you ordered me to leave and, when I walked out the door, I intended doing exactly that. I'd actually reached Kentucky before Dad and I stopped for a bite of breakfast." He took a breather, mostly to gauge Ann's reaction to his statement that he'd really planned to leave. He felt wonderful satisfaction from her unhappy expression.

"It was for the best," she cried softly. "You should've kept going. Why didn't you?"

Jack recognized her defensive position. She sat poker straight in her chair with her knees pressed together. Her fingers picked at the fabric of her overalls, and her face projected a picture of misery. Her body language gave Jack the only hope he possessed.

"I'd already made up my mind I would be back in a few days before I even reached the Hummer. I came back today because of something I saw at the restaurant in Kentucky. I saw a picture taken back in the early thirties of a black man hanging from a wooden gallows." Jack watched her skin turn white again and nodded his head. "The caption read 'Black

Man Hanged for Killing a White Man.' Suddenly everything clicked into place. I knew what the missing ingredient had been all along. How could Haber Judd be released from the hospital in just one day if he'd been injured so badly he couldn't come to the house and help you the night Red died? He must have had a miraculous recovery." Ann jumped up from her chair so fast and hard that it flew backward and crashed on the floor.

"Get out," she cried so loud that Peanut came bounding into the house. "You have to leave!" The order became a plea as Ann surged into a panic. Hadn't she known all along that Jack wouldn't stop until he solved the puzzle? She must convince him to go back to Indiana. Now! "Please, Jack, please go home. I'll give your company my land if you'll j-just g-go h-h-home." She had started sobbing by now. Jack felt like the worst kind of low life. He couldn't stand seeing Ann so distressed and had become resigned to giving up, when the door opened wider and Haber Judd entered the room. Jack settled carefully back into the chair he'd half risen from and waited.

"No Mam, ain't gonna let ya do it." The old man spoke quietly in a room silent except for Ann's sobs. "Be time, and past, we put this muddle ta rest."

Ann put her hand up to command silence, but nobody paid the least attention.

"Are you finally ready to talk, Haber Judd?" Jack asked the proud black man. He turned toward Jack with an uncommon air of defeat. He seemed to have aged twenty years since he held that shotgun out in the garden patch. Jack mourned the loss, but he expected it would be temporary.

"Ah 'spect ya already figgered out Ah kilt the rattler." Haber Judd made a rude sound. "Ain't nobody more deservin' a dyin' than that snake in the grass." In the background, Ann begged him to stay silent, assuring him he didn't have to tell Jack anything, but the die was cast.

"Tell me," Jack prompted.

"Ya already seen them pitchers," Haber Judd continued. "He wuz gonna kill 'er. Ah heered 'er cryin' and beggin' rat from the start. Ya wuz rat about that. Ah heered it all. But it took me a powerful long time ta git up here ta the house. Ah had ta crawl, and Ah did'n do that real good. Ah pulled mahself in through the kitchen and found 'is shotgun leanin' up agin' the wall baside the door ta the livin' room whur he had 'er. Ah had ta hunt out the shells. He wuz so busy hurtin' the Mam, he did'n even see me loadin' the gun rat behind 'em." Haber Judd paused to gather his thoughts for only a moment before he continued with the gruesome tale.

"When Ah got the bullets loaded, Ah wuz only meanin' ta threaten 'em, but when 'e saw Ah had 'is gun, he kicked out at me. 'Is big ole boot caught me in the neck." Haber Judd put a finger on his Adam's apple. "At's why Ah talk lack a ole buzz saw. People at the hospital said Ah wuz lucky ta have any voice a'tall. Anyways, when 'e kicked me, the gun went off. Ah reckon it wuz pointed rat up at 'is face."

Ann came and stood beside Haber Judd like a bodyguard.

She placed her hand on his shoulder and glared at Jack through tear stained eyes. If looks could kill…

"Why didn't the investigators figure that out from the crime scene?" Jack asked. That was another puzzle piece that still hadn't fallen into place.

"Member Ah told ya, the Mam's real smart." Haber Judd actually chuckled. "She wuz barely awake, but she said they'd hang me if'n Ah wuz caught, said Ah had ta hide the fact Ah'd been in the house. She said for me ta smear thangs around, so's Ah looked real good and made sure ever hinkerin' of me wuz gone. Then Ah pulled 'er ta the door over mah tracks so's nobody could tell Ah'd been here. She said ta take off the bloody clothes 'n mess up mah tracks back ta the chicken house. She give me a pair a pants an' a ole shirt, so's Ah buried them bloody thangs under mah pallet. Later we burned 'um. Took me all night ta do whut she said. Ah wuz plum tuckered out." The old black man looked plum tuckered out now, as well, Jack thought.

"Where was Peanut?" Jack asked, knowing the dog would've been in the middle of any attack on Ann like a flea on his own back.

"The first thing Red did was hit him over the head," Ann said, patting her faithful protector on his big fuzzy noggin. "I thought he'd killed him, but Peanut had only passed out and when he came to, he actually helped in our deception by running all around me, and Red's body, too, and messing up any evidence that Haber Judd might have missed."

"I don't see the problem," Jack told them in a truly baffled tone. "Red's death was an accident. Surely the evidence would have borne that out." Jack came in for yet another surprise.

"It's plain as the nose on your face you don't know beans about the way things are done in the south—leastwise around here." Ann sneered at Jack's ignorance. "If the police had known what Haber Judd did, do you think they would've worried that he tried to save my life? Do you really believe they would've cared that the gun fired on its own? No," she shouted, "they would've seen a black man who had killed a white man, and he'd be sitting on death row right now!" Her voice rose steadily throughout her speech until she was yelling. Her face turned red and her chest heaved.

Jack became very excited.

"And you think we should leave things the way they are?" Jack asked, exerting an effort to keep from smiling with the happiness bursting inside him. He looked back at the man who'd just confessed to causing the death of another human being—that human part being questionable. "What do you think, Haber Judd?"

"Ah reckon Ah'm goin' off ta jail," he answered as he dropped his eyes, missing the tiny shake of Jack's head. "'Bout time, Ah 'spect. Never meant the Mam ta suffer fer som'um Ah done. Ah be goin' off ta the sheriff now." Haber Judd started to stand.

"Sit down," Jack ordered and Haber Judd did, probably

expecting another bout of questions. "You are the bravest man I've ever known," Jack murmured, then he looked at Ann. "You've been blessed with a true friend." Both Ann's and Haber Judd's mouths were hanging open in shock.

"I know," Ann finally squeaked out.

"And you, Haber Judd," Jack said to the man who sat staring at him. Haber Judd's eyes communicated things the man himself couldn't put into words, like *thank you* and *don't hurt Ann*, and *take care of her for me when I'm not here.* "You've been blessed with a wonderful friend as well. I hope you'll count me as your friend, too." Haber Judd nodded and started to rise again.

"Jack!" Ann cried, and he could hear the plea in her voice. At that moment, he realized they didn't understand what he meant to do. He stood and crossed the small space that separated him from the three of them. He extended his hand to Haber Judd, who looked first at the hand, and then into Jack's eyes. Haber Judd raised his and they shook, but Jack didn't let go.

"I'm not saying a word and neither are you," Jack murmured as they stood eye to eye. He waited the minute it took Haber Judd to absorb that statement, and then he continued. "I'm not as ignorant of the ways of the old south as you may think." His love filled gaze turned to Ann. "I wouldn't take a chance with Haber Judd's life for anything. Besides," he said looking back to Haber Judd, "if I helped send you to jail, even for one day, Ann would never marry me."

Ann squealed with delight and threw herself at Jack in an unusual display of exuberance. She hugged him so tight he thought a rib might crack. He loved being the recipient of her affection and hugged her right back. Peanut danced around them, jumping up and down like an excited child. Jack glanced in Haber Judd's direction. The man stood with his hand still in Jack's, looking for all the world like he didn't understand a thing that had just happened.

Ann spun around and, for the second time ever, threw her arms around Haber Judd. Jack could have laughed at the expression of shock and anxiety on the older man's face. When their eyes met over her shoulder, Jack recognized Haber Judd's apprehension, but instead of warning Ann away, he actually joined the clutch by putting his arms around them both. Haber Judd's look of astonishment made all the worry Jack carried while he waited for them to come clean almost worthwhile.

After the emotional chaos diminished and their hearts had settled once more into a steady rhythm, the three humans made a solemn vow never to tell a single soul about Haber Judd's part in Red Mason's death. Jack felt humbled by the gratitude in the other man's eyes and the loyalty in his attitude.

They'd missed supper, so Jack offered to pick up pizza. The blank looks on both their faces told him they'd never shared a slice. He couldn't wait to introduce them to this new treat. He intended making sure there would be many more treats in their future. He felt like Santa Claus.

After they'd dined on the newly discovered wonder of sausage and pepperoni cooked with tomato sauce on a thin slice of dough, they cleaned the kitchen and Ann read from the Bible.

This time, Jack noticed her incomplete education, and he recognized the charming hesitations when she pronounced her words as uncertainty. He instinctively knew her lack of confidence would be a problem between them. Later in the barn, he put his brain to work on solving that particular monster before it raised its ugly head.

The next morning, they rose and started their day as if nothing had happened. Jack helped Haber Judd feed and water the animals, and they washed up before going inside to enjoy the food Ann had prepared. After they finished, Jack cornered Ann and insisted they talk.

Chapter 12

"You never gave me an answer to the question I asked you yesterday," he said as he moved in closer to put his hands on her waist and his lips on her mouth.

Ann's heart began pounding like an Indian war drum. A fever invaded her body, and she found herself yearning to caress him. She couldn't fathom the wonderful feeling she experienced whenever he touched her.

Before Jack ended the kiss his temperature had reached an uncomfortable level, but he wasn't complaining. He loved it. He loved her. He lifted his lips and looked deep into her dreamy eyes.

"Well?" he asked. "Will you marry me?" The dreaminess faded slowly, replaced by wariness.

"I can't," she murmured miserably.

"Why?" he cried. "You love me, don't you?" But a note of insecurity crept into his voice.

"Oh, yes!" She began reassuring him quickly. "I love you,

Jack. You know I do."

Jack breathed a sigh of relief. She'd finally said the words he'd begun fearing he would never hear. "So what's the problem? We'll marry, have a dozen little Jacks and Anns and live happily ever after."

Ann's eyes grew misty. She'd never let herself seriously consider having children; now Jack had brought to life a full blown dream of sandy haired little girls and chocolate eyed little boys. But the dream remained one she couldn't have. She must try and explain to him the impossibility. She put some distance between them so she could marshal her thoughts.

"You paint a beautiful picture," she said, eyeing him with sadness, "but we live worlds apart."

She didn't know it, but her eyes were telling him something else. They were saying this was the hardest thing she'd ever done. They were saying he offered what she wanted more than anything else in the world. Jack smiled.

"Ann, just think of the beautiful sight when worlds collide."

She had already started shaking her head. "It's an explosion, Jack. Everything blows to bits." The words came out jerky from a catch in her voice. "I don't want us to blow up. I won't fit into your world, and you won't fit into mine. Maybe you could visit once in a while?" She had such hope in her voice he wanted to shake her.

"Is that all you think you're worth? You're willing to settle for a hole in the wall affair?" Jack bristled. "Well, I'm not.

I want the whole enchilada." Ann's face took on a mulish look. Jack decided she wasn't going to tell him what really banned her from becoming his wife, so he'd have to tell her. "You think we can't marry because you haven't received enough schooling to cope with my lifestyle?" he asked.

Ann widened her eyes and her mouth opened and closed three times before she could answer. "No!" she practically shouted, bringing Peanut instantly to her side. "I...well...you...I guess that might...how did you know?" She stopped stuttering long enough to inquire, absentmindedly rubbing Peanut's ears as she waited for Jack's answer.

"I wouldn't have known on my own," he said a bit smugly. "I had help."

"Haber Judd," she said indignantly, and Jack laughed out loud at the annoyed look on her face.

"I know how to solve that problem," he told her, tongue in cheek. Ann's eyes widened even more with interest. "We'll go to Indiana so you can meet my parents. If you like them, which you will," he uttered with great confidence, "you can stay with them and attend school until I finish here. When I come home, we'll be married, and you can continue with your education for as long as you want." He tried reading her expression, but he'd never seen that look before. Her face showed a mixture of excitement, anticipation, fear, love, hope, joy...too many emotions to identify.

"I...don't know," Ann said, hardly aware of the words she spoke. "Do you think they'd like me? No," she kept talking, not letting him answer. "I couldn't put them in that position. Jack, you can't ask them to bring a stranger into their home. I'd be an embarrassment. No, your plan wouldn't work…"

He finally had to kiss her to shut her up. By the time he finished, they were both so muddled they couldn't think for a minute.

"Let's go find out," Jack muttered, realizing he had trouble keeping his head around this woman, and feeling smug because he regained his senses before Ann regained hers.

"I can't leave my home," she cried a little desperately. "And Peanut," she added, looking down at her loving animal friend. "And Haber Judd," she included in her growing list. Jack now had yet another glitch to solve. He thought for only a moment before presenting a solution for every one of her concerns.

"We'll take care of Haber Judd," Jack answered positively. "He can come with us if he wants. We'll take Peanut, too. That goes without saying." He put his finger under her chin and lifted her face until she stared into his chocolate eyes. "You don't have any other close friends you would hate to leave, do you?" She shook her head. He understood she shook it in refusal of everything he offered.

"I can't," she whispered and exposed the other big problem. "I've never been out of the state of Tennessee, actually no farther than Knoxville. I wouldn't know how to act." She became upset again. Jack pulled her close and held her until she calmed.

"I know it's a big change," he said quietly. "I'll help you every step of the way, and if you reach a point where you can't stand living in Indiana, so be it. I'll bring you home, and we'll live here." She jerked back and looked into his face, scrutinizing him intently.

"You'd do that for me?" she whispered. "You'd uproot you life and come and live here...for me?" The words trembled from her lips in awe, her face glowed with love.

Jack grew thrilled at the wonder she displayed. "I would, if it became necessary, but I hope you'll at least try my way first." He searched every nuance of her expression, and thought he spotted a flicker of curiosity. That gave him courage enough to throw his best sales pitch.

"Look upon expanding your education as a great adventure. Think of the move as the beginning of a new life. You're leaving the old one behind to start an exciting journey. But it'll be a journey without danger, because I'll make sure you're protected." He looked down at the big fur ball leaning against his leg and amended his statement. "Me and Peanut." He heard a joyful cry, and she flung her arms around his neck.

Inside Ann's chest, a rusty lock had just clicked open and a prisoner escaped. She felt the first tentative steps toward freedom, and knew a moment's terror at the thought of leaving her heart exposed, vulnerable to hurt.

"I'm afraid," she cried softly into his neck.

"So am I," he countered. "I'm afraid of losing you. I need you," he whispered fervently, "more than air, because without you I'd have nothing to live for. I'd probably go on existing, but what would be the point? Don't ever leave me."

Ann heard an order and a plea all rolled up in one. She drew back and looked at him again.

He saw fear in her eyes and determination as well. Jack held his breath, sweating those same egg-sized pellets, as he waited to see which would win.

"All right," Ann said after an eternity.

She inhaled to continue, but he squeezed the air right back out of her. Then they were both laughing and crying as he picked her up off the floor and twirled her around with Peanut jumping and barking enthusiastically.

Calming down and continuing with their usual tasks took a while. Ann finally dashed outside to help Haber Judd finish the late garden planting. Jack headed for the site and conferred with Dan Weaver about his change in plans and duties.

Both of them managed to function all day, doing their jobs with their usual ability, but underneath the everyday labors, they were connected with each other through their thoughts and emotions. They never really felt separated.

When quitting time arrived, they made for Ann's kitchen like homing pigeons. Ann washed from head to toe. Jack cleaned up in record time and hurried in to help Ann cook supper. They both took pleasure in the new experience.

They all ate with enjoyment and congeniality and cleaned up together. After the two men sat and listened while Ann read, Haber Judd left for the barn. At last, the two lovebirds were alone. They talked long into the night and finally, worn out from the mental and emotional strain of the extra long day, they fell asleep on Ann's bed.

When Jack awoke the next morning, the strange bedroom confused him, but the mouth-watering aroma floating in the air told him Ann was cooking breakfast. He arose and wandered into the kitchen to hug the cook, after which he trotted out to the barn for his early morning sponge bath. There he met the intent, disapproving stare of Haber Judd.

"We're getting married," Jack told him before he had a chance to blow his stack, and went on to explain they'd talked until the wee hours of the morning and fell asleep. Haber Judd was mollified.

At the table, while they enjoyed a breakfast feast of bacon, eggs, grits, biscuits, and strong coffee, they talked about the changes that would soon come.

After a complete explanation, Haber Judd agreed to stay on and take care of Ann's property while she traveled north with Jack to meet his family. If everything proceeded according to plan, she might stay and go to school. The huge smile Haber Judd wore throughout the entire meal told both Ann and Jack how happy he felt with their arrangements.

Later that morning, Jack drove into Andersonville and made a very expensive long-distance call to his parents. First he talked with Wilma for thirty minutes, and then he talked with Mike for thirty minutes. After that, they used extensions and he talked to both of them for another twenty minutes. By the time they'd talked until their throats hurt, everything was settled. Ann would be invited to stay with them.

But they hadn't just rolled over for him as they always had in the past. They asked some hard questions, like what her background consisted of. He related the story of Red's death, and grudgingly told them some of the locals suspected she killed her husband. Telling Wilma and Mike that part proved hard for Jack, but he wanted them to have all the facts. He didn't want anything coming up and biting him on the butt later. "Reserve judgment until you come to know her. I know you'll love her as much as I do." His request put them on the spot. His pride in his parents mushroomed when they reluctantly agreed.

They also asked how he could be so sure she was the woman he wanted to spend the rest of his life with when he'd known her such a short time. "I can't answer that, I just know," he told them. "I can only ask, once again, that you reserve judgment because I know for certain you'll understand when you meet her."

Wilma and Mike had serious reservations, but when they hung up from speaking with Jack, they decided the marriage would be a grand affair if she proved half as good as Jack thought. They would welcome her into their home.

He made several more calls and when he finished, he left the store whistling.

The next day Jack insisted on taking Ann and Haber Judd into Knoxville. He endured a lot of argument, but Jack won in the end. He maintained Haber Judd had earned a shopping trip for all the hard work he'd put in here over the years. He claimed Ann must have different clothes for the life she intended to start, and as his wife, it became his responsibility—and privilege—to feed and clothe her.

So with reservations, Ann and Haber Judd started on their exciting journey. She'd been to Knoxville many times through the years to peddle her carvings, but this time seemed different. She rode as a passenger, able to freely observe all the wonders of the outer world. She became entranced.

Haber Judd was just plain scared. The last few years he'd lived in Knoxville, he existed in an alcohol induced haze. He hadn't been back since those boys hauled him away. Nothing looked familiar until Jack pulled up in front of an apartment building in a questionable neighborhood.

"At's Molly's buildin'," Haber Judd said, recognizing the address and sitting straight up. "Whut we doin' heah?"

Jack killed the engine and turned to face the other man. "I took the liberty of calling on Molly and asking if she'd see you," Jack told his friend. "She told me she never stopped loving you, Haber Judd. She says if you've given up the bottle, and you want her, she'll gladly take you back." Haber Judd looked stunned. His brain seemed to have ceased functioning. Jack grew worried. "Did I do wrong?" he questioned.

Haber Judd shook his head and, with tears running down his old leathered cheeks, he climbed out of the Hummer and lurched inside.

Ann and Jack waited. An hour later, a younger looking

man came out of the building and jumped back in the truck. He laughed as he told them his wife and kids had been waiting with open arms. One of his babies had married and had children of her own, making him a grandpa. His son had a good job and a nice apartment. Molly said she would come to Norris and live with him while Ann stayed with the Barrister's. If Ann decided not to stay in Indiana, Haber Judd and Molly would find another place close by.

Jack told him not to worry about that, because if Ann didn't want to stay with his parents and attend school, they would build a bigger house anyway.

One year later, Jack and Ann were married. In that year a lot happened. Jack finished his work in Tennessee and returned home a changed man. Ann received a high school diploma and signed up for college classes. Haber Judd reunited with his family and moved Molly into Ann's cabin. He started working for the resort Barrister's built. Life was good.

Ann overflowed with so much joy it hurt. She never knew a life like the one she had now was possible. Mike and Wilma fell in love with her almost immediately, and she and Peanut settled into their home like they belonged. Betsy, Ann's new sister-in-law, became her first ever female friend.

Best of all was Jack! Every day, every hour, she thanked God for him. He had become her reason for living. Now her life felt almost complete, and would be as soon as they had their own little Jacks and Anns.

ABOUT THE AUTHOR

Violet L Ryan, author of *Tennessee Moonlight*, has created stories all her life. Between authoring several books, she's written articles for newspapers and Christian communications. Short stories published in *Weeds Corner Magazine* include "Rachel's Return to Christmas", "Santa's Swan Song", "Blackjack", "The Snake Slayer", and "Family Treasure", along with the occasional poem. She regularly participates in Midwest Writer's Workshops and belongs to Writers Ink of Central Indiana. Violet loves the small Midwestern town where she and hubby, Denny, raised their three beautiful daughters. Favorite pastimes include eating out with friends after Sunday morning church, painting, drawing, reading, and writing.

For your reading pleasure, we invite you to visit our web bookstore

WHISKEY CREEK PRESS

www.whiskeycreekpress.com